Haja's Call

J.D. Pujals

Contents

Dedication

To all those who find magic in the ordinary, beauty in the imperfect, and truth in the unknown. May this book inspire you to embrace your own uniqueness and find peace in connection with nature and the universe.

Acknowledgements

To my most beloved one, my cat, whose presence has filled my life with joy and unconditional companionship, he has been the purest manifestation of infinite love.

To my chosen family and friends, who have been my rock and my inspiration throughout this journey. Your unconditional love and constant support have been my light in the dark times and my source of joy when I have needed it the most.

To nature and the beauty of earth, which have inspired me with their grandeur and majesty. Every sunrise, every sunset, and every encounter with wildlife has fed my spirit and nourished my soul.

To the universe, for its mysteries and wonders, for its lessons and its blessings. In every star in the sky, in every breath of wind, and in every heartbeat of the galaxy, I have found the magic and wisdom I sought.

To the readers, whose curiosity and passion for exploration have brought these pages to life. May this literary journey take you to places of wonder and reflection, and may you find in these words a refuge for your imagination and your spirit.

About the Author

J.D. Pujals (born May 16, 1984, in Santo Domingo, Dominican Republic) is a multifaceted Canadian artist. Renowned as a painter, sculptor and writer, his work reflects a fusion of the figurative and the abstract, infused with a mystical touch and a deep connection with nature.

From an early age, he showed an innate inclination toward art and writing, exploring the intersections between the human mind, the universe, and magic. His literary style, inspired by Latin American magical realism, is characterized by its relaxed, casual, and lighthearted tone, which invites internal reflection and the search for each individual's purpose in life.

J.D. Pujals' educational and professional background is as diverse as his art. At the age of 6, he moved to the United States, where he was exposed to a new culture and outlook on life. This early experience enriched his worldview and contributed to the formation of his artistic identity. Subsequently, he returned to the Dominican Republic to continue his studies. He graduated with a degree in advertising, a discipline that, along with his exposure to Dominican culture, influenced his understanding of visual communication and storytelling, aspects that he would later integrate into his art.

Following his training in advertising, he ventured to Chile, where the region's rich cultural diversity and artistic effervescence further stimulated his creativity. He decided to study industrial design in Spain, thus exploring new aesthetic and conceptual dimensions that would be reflected in his work. After completing his training, he returned from Spain to Chile, where he worked as a teacher of English as a second language for several years, working for one of the largest pharmaceutical companies in the world.

He later moved to Canada, where he currently lives. He is deeply influenced by the landscapes, cultural diversity, and society's commitment to environmental protection and animal rights. This experience marked a significant change in his life, leading him to adopt a plant-based lifestyle, which he incorporates into his writings through a strong message of environmental awareness and respect for all forms of life.

His art has been exhibited and recognized internationally, highlighting its ability to evoke emotions and awaken people's imagination. His commitment to exploring the human soul and promoting happiness and fulfillment is reflected in both his art and his words, demonstrating that the true purpose of life lies in living in harmony with oneself and the world around us.

J.D. Pujals' work transcends borders and cultures, inspiring others to seek beauty and meaning in every moment of life and the magic all around us.

Epigraph

"Happiness is our main purpose in this life, and to be happy, we must look beyond the ordinary. It is in that place where the magic and wisdom of the universe converge, where the keys are hidden in plain sight in the nature that surrounds us, waiting to be discovered by those who seek with open hearts."

Preface

On the winding journey of Maple Pelridge, we enter a world where the boundaries between reality and fantasy are blurred and where every encounter and every experience reveal deeper layers of the human soul. From the lush landscapes of Marina Willows to the mysterious paths of Haja Island, we follow in Maple's footsteps in her search for identity, meaning and inner peace.

In this story, we find a gallery of characters as fascinating as they are mysterious: from the enigmatic Mister Universe, who personifies the very essence of creation, to the mystical presence of Haja, the personification of nature and life itself. Through these encounters, Maple immerses herself in an introspective journey where reality merges with fantasy and where the boundaries of time and space fade away.

Every page of this story is a window into Maple's inner world, where dreams and visions are intertwined with finding answers and battling her inner demons. From moments of despair to glimmers of hope, Maple invites us to explore the abysses of the human mind and discover the true nature of reality.

Through this journey, we are immersed in an ocean of emotions and reflections, where every word is an echo of the eternal search of the human being to understand its place in the universe. Get ready to embark on a journey full of mystery, magic, and self-discovery, where truth lies in the depths of the soul and where every breath is another step toward inner enlightenment.

Introduction

Surrounded by forests, among ancient trees and crystal-clear streams, in a picturesque little city resides a woman whose soul is intertwined with the very essence of nature. Her name is Maple Pelridge, and her life is soaked in mysticism, magic, and a deep connection to the cosmos.

A talented artist in every way, Maple finds her inspiration in the untamed beauty that surrounds her. From her earliest days, she has felt an inexplicable attraction to the supernatural and the unknown, finding solace and marvel in the wonders of the natural world.

But Maple's life is marked by extraordinary encounters and visions that defy conventional logic. Years ago, she had a mystical encounter with a celestial entity called Mister Universe, whose ancient wisdom and luminous presence left her amazed and forever transformed. Since then, Maple has felt an intimate connection to Mister Universe, firmly believing in his existence and the messages he conveys to her.

However, her conviction is met with doubt and skepticism from others. Psychologists and psychiatrists suggest that Maple's encounters with Mister Universe are mere figments of her imagination, attributing them to a possible bipolar condition. Even her sister, Honey, concerned for her well-being, insists that Maple continue to take the prescribed medications.

But Maple is convinced of the truth of her experiences. Her obsession with the beauty of nature and her connection to Mister

Universe led her to explore her own spiritual path, defying conventional explanations and seeking understanding in the deepest corners of the world.

Meanwhile, her best friend Julie and Julie's mother, Dinorah, a psychologist specializing in puppet therapy, offer support and unique perspectives on her journey. Through the unlikely friendship between Julie and Honey, Maple finds a wider circle of support and an unexpected connection that defies family barriers.

At the heart of it all, the beauty of nature and a love of animals guide Maple in her search for meaning and truth. Despite the doubts and challenges she faces, Maple bravely forges forward, relying on her intuition and the wisdom of Mister Universe to find her way in the world.

Thus continues the story of Maple Pelridge, a story of mysticism, magic, and the soul's eternal quest for truth and understanding in a vast and mysterious universe.

Chapter 1: Waking Up Early

A throaty meow cut through the morning air, breaking Maple's peaceful sleep. One after another, the meows continued relentlessly, announcing that the rest had come to an end. Maple blinked, feeling the weight of drowsiness as she checked her watch. It was barely 6:12 in the morning.

Maple was on duty taking care of Bagel, her best friend Julie's lovely cat, who was enjoying a well-deserved vacation in Europe. Recently, Maple had installed grow lights for her plants, scheduled to activate at 6 o'clock. However, for some mysterious reason, the lights would come on a bit late, at 6:11 a.m.

Maple's roommate, Ria, had already left for work at the public library, leaving Maple with the unusual early awakening. Although Maple longed to stay in bed for a few more minutes, Bagel's persistence in his meows forced her to get up.

With a resigned sigh, Maple headed for the bathroom. Out of the corner of her eye, she saw Bagel's claw peeking through the semi open door, indicating that the mischievous feline was not giving up. Maple carefully opened the door to make way for him.

After tending to morning necessities in the bathroom, Maple headed to the kitchen. Her faithful companion, Pancake, lay asleep in one of the many beds Maple had arranged for him. Opening the refrigerator, Maple pulled out a packet of plant-based, enriched cat food, Bagel's insatiable appetite was showing no signs of stopping his meows. Maple finally served him the food, and he devoured it eagerly.

Deciding to take advantage of the early morning, Maple reached for Pancake's strap. The sound of the metal buckle clashing echoed through the room, waking the dog from his slumber. Pancake, full of joy, began to spin and stood in front of the door, eager to begin his morning walk. As Bagel continued to enjoy his breakfast, Maple prepared to enjoy the cool sunrise alongside her loyal canine companion.

Chapter 2: Hello Again

Maple fastened Pancake's strap dexterously as Bagel continued his feast in the kitchen. With a gentle tug, Pancake signaled to Maple that he was ready to go. Opening the door carefully, Maple and Pancake stepped out into the crisp morning air, heading for Marina Willows Park, Maple's favorite place.

The sun was just beginning to peek over the trees, weaving delicate shadows on the ground. Maple took a deep breath of the fresh, perfumed air, letting the morning energy envelop her.

The silence of the morning was broken only by the sounds of nature awakening around them. The chirping of birds and the soft whisper of the wind through the leaves of the trees created a harmonious symphony that accompanied the steps of Maple and Pancake.

They walked in silence, enjoying the tranquility of the morning and each other's company. Pancake curiously sniffed around every bush and tree in his path while Maple let her thoughts wander freely, absorbed in the beauty of her surroundings.

Suddenly, a flash of light caught her attention. Maple looked up to see a ray of sunlight filtering through the branches of an old oak tree, illuminating a small clearing in the woods. In the center of this light, something shone with a mysterious, glowing light.

Intrigued, Maple walked over with Pancake by her side. As they entered the clearing, the light intensified, enveloping them in a warm, comforting glow. Maple felt a strange sense of curiosity and wonder wash over her as she approached the source of the light.

Then, Maple stared directly at the sun for a fleeting instant. Strange symbols imprinted themselves in her mind, and she heard the voice of Mister Universe, whom she hadn't heard of since she began her antipsychotic treatment.

"Maple," the voice whispered, echoing in the depths of her consciousness. "It's been so long since we've spoken directly. I've missed you."

Maple was overwhelmed by the intensity of the experience. Mister Universe's words filled her with a sense of nostalgia and relief as if she was reconnecting with an old friend after a long time.

At that moment, Maple knew that her encounter with Mister Universe had not been a dream or wishful thinking but a reaffirmation of the deep connection they shared. As the sun slowly ascended in the sky, Maple and Pancake continued on their way through Marina Willows Park, enveloped in the light and magic of the universe around them.

Chapter 3: Secrets

As Maple walked along with Pancake on the tree-lined path of Marina Willows Park, a voice echoed in her mind, clear and resonant. It was Mister Universe again, confessing to her a series of secrets that had been hidden for a millennium.

"Maple," Mister Universe whispered, "there are things that the world is not yet ready to understand. That's why these secrets must remain between the two of us."

Maple stopped in her tracks, stunned by Mister Universe's revelations. A torrent of emotions and thoughts rushed into her mind as she struggled to process what she had just heard. She longed to share these revelations with her best friend Julie, but before she could even consider it, Mister Universe warned her, "I can't stop you from doing anything. You will know how to handle the information I have revealed to you today."

Maple recalled the moments spent with Mister Universe, moments that had marked her life forever. Despite the medications she took, which tried to quell the intensity of her experiences, Maple had always kept alive the flame of her belief in what she had experienced.

She recalled the day she first saw Mister Universe's colossal eyes in the sea off Marina Willows. Back then, Mister Universe had asked her what she wanted most in life, and before she could answer, he had whispered, "Do you want the suffering of the world to end?" Then, he revealed a cryptic message: "10:25." Maple had never fully grasped the meaning of that riddle, but now, years later, she still couldn't crack it.

Among the secrets revealed by Mister Universe, many questions arose, but perhaps the most important was the meaning of "10:25." However, Mister Universe hadn't revealed this mystery among the three shared secrets. Maple was overwhelmed by uncertainty.

"Why are you looking for me again now?" asked Maple, desperate for answers. "Last time, everyone thought I was crazy, and you had warned me. I know, I didn't listen to you."

Mister Universe calmly replied, "Maple, the three secrets I have revealed to you contain all the answers to all your questions. By the way, it's been a while since you've used your divination cards. Maybe they'll help you find the answers you're looking for, and don't forget…West is best."

With one last farewell message, Mister Universe vanished from Maple's mind, leaving her in a sea of thoughts and emotions. Maple felt more determined than ever to unravel the mysteries around her, and Mister Universe's words echoed in her mind as she continued on her way alongside Pancake.

"By the way," Mister Universe added in his farewell, "Pancake wants you to know that to him, you're everything, too. See you later."

Maple nodded, comforted by Mister Universe's words and the unconditional support of her faithful canine companion. She knew her path was full of challenges and unanswered questions, but she was determined to find the truth she longed for.

So, Maple continued her walk through Marina Willows Park, ready to face whatever fate had in store for her and find the answers she was looking for.

Chapter 4: Sigh

Maple walked alongside Pancake, still overwhelmed by Mister Universe's revelations. Suddenly, she stopped in her tracks and said to herself, "Maple, maybe you're going crazy. Maybe you are, in fact, bipolar."

With a heavy sigh, Maple decided to return home. She put on her headphones and chose to listen to her favorite band, Sky Water, in an attempt to calm her turbulent thoughts. Maple and Pancake arrived home, where Bagel was waiting for them in front of the entrance, meowing incessantly.

"Your meows are really driving me crazy!" joked Maple, chuckling. "It looks like I'm really losing my mind."

Maple walked to her small office in the room, where her computer was located. Despite being an established online influencer, Maple recalled how her life had taken a radical turn since she met Mister Universe in the past. She had quit her job at a call center, where her younger sister, Honey, was her direct boss, to pursue her dream of connecting with millions of people through her social media platforms.

Although she had achieved much success since then, today, despite all her exploits, Maple felt truly uneasy. Mister Universe's last message had left her thinking: Had Pancake really expressed his feelings through Mister Universe, or was it just a sign that Maple was losing her sanity again?

Maple looked at her computer, which was flooded with thousands of notifications as usual since she went viral on social media. Despite her success, Maple remained humble and unassuming, using her earnings to help her mother, Pearl, and stepfather, Lars.

"It makes me want to tell Mom and Julie," Maple said quietly, feeling a knot of anxiety in her stomach. "But I'm afraid to scare them". She decided to call Julie anyway.

With a purposeful move, Maple grabbed her phone and dialed Julie's number, ready to share her worries with her best friend and trust her as she always had.

Chapter 5: I've Heard Him Again

"Hello, Maple. What's up?" replied Julie on the phone.

"Julie," Maple began with a sigh, "I don't know if I should tell you what happened today when I went for a walk with Pancake."

"You don't have to tell me anything you're not comfortable with," Julie said sympathetically.

"I know, Julie, but I know you're on vacation, and I don't want to worry you," Maple replied.

Julie was immediately alarmed. "Has something happened to Bagel? Tell me, and if I have to change my flights, I'll be back today."

"No, Julie, Bagel is happy and content. He gets along really well with Pancake even though they're a dog and a cat, as you know," Maple explained.

"Then why do you say you don't want to worry me? Has something happened to you?" asked Julie worriedly. "You know I'd change my flight for you, too."

"No, Julie, you don't have to. It's just that I miss you, and well, I also think I've had another episode of psychosis," Maple confessed candidly.

Julie was instantly worried. "But Maple, you've always said you don't think you're bipolar. What made you think you're losing your sanity?"

"I've heard him again," Maple replied in a trembling voice. "Mister Universe".

Julie was silent for a moment, processing the information. "I'm going to change my flight to return as soon as possible," she announced decisively.

"No need, Julie," Maple insisted.

"You won't change my mind," Julie replied determinedly. "See you soon. I have to go now. I love you."

"I love you too," Maple replied with a lump in her throat as she hung up the phone.

With a sigh, Maple lay on her bed, overwhelmed by the mix of emotions that invaded her. She knew she would have to face this situation bravely, and with Julie's support by her side, she felt a little bit stronger.

Chapter 6: Disbelief

As Maple lay on the bed, lost in her thoughts, Pancake walked over and lay down beside her. Maple gently stroked his fur and began to speak softly.

"Pancake, I don't know if what Mister Universe told me is true, but for me, there is no being I love more than you. Yes, I love my mother and sister, and I love Julie, and there are many people I love, but you, Pancake, are my life. I was born to find you, and I know I'm not your real mother. It hurts me that you don't know your own birth mother, but I live for you, and I will give you all the love I have inside, even though I am losing my mind."

Pancake looked into her eyes with his trademark doggy smile and his tongue sticking out, filling the air with joy. Just then, the phone rang. The screen showed Honey's name.

"I wonder what Honey wants," Maple muttered to herself. "I'm not ready to face her. She's always thought I'm crazy, and that's one of the reasons I keep taking antipsychotics, which don't even seem to work because I'm going crazy anyway."

Maple took a deep breath and answered the call. "Hello, Honey."

Honey spoke with concern in her voice. "Maple, I talked to Julie on the phone, and she told me you had another episode. I've already called Dr. Goldbucket, but she wasn't there. I left her a message with her secretary."

Maple felt a surge of anger and frustration. "I don't want to talk about it now," she replied firmly. The thought that Julie had shared such personal information with Honey bothered her deeply.

Honey tried to reassure her. "Maple, believe it or not, I have your best interests in mind. Don't make this harder than it needs to be. We'll talk later."

Maple hung up the phone with a heavy sigh. She felt betrayed and hurt by Julie's lack of confidentiality. A sense of frustration washed over her, and she wondered if she could ever trust anyone completely again.

With Pancake still by her side, Maple sank into a state of melancholy, wondering what the future would hold and whether she would ever find peace and stability in her tumultuous life.

Chapter 7: The First Call

Maple was still in a state of melancholy and confusion. She clearly remembered not only the recent events with the ray of light but also how the whole story began: how she met Mister Universe. It was a few years ago when Maple was going through a severe depression. Her relationship with Jonah was over, a decision she knew was right, but the breakup was not the only reason for her sadness. It all had to do with her childhood and her father, Roman's cousin, Darius.

Maple closed her eyes and remembered everything with pain. She felt broken, but she knew she wasn't alone. There was Pancake and her best friend Julie. Her sister Honey was also present, though Maple did not know it yet.

At one of the girls' nights with Julie, which became a beacon of hope for Maple's mental health, Julie not only gave Maple her ears, advice, and friendship but also one of her vegan wild berry smoothies. Julie used to pick the berries at Marina Willows Park.

After that night, Maple decided to go to Marina Willows Park, this time without her dog Pancake. While there, she felt a strong urge to pick berries. Suddenly, her own voice echoed in her head, telling her, "Head to the Fairy Forest."

The "Fairy Forest" was a place in the park full of dense trees and shrubs with a magical atmosphere. People from town affectionately called it the enchanted forest. Maple was on a day off from work, so she decided to follow the call of her inner voice.

With determined steps, Maple made her way into the woods, feeling a mixture of excitement and nervousness. She didn't know what she would find there, but she was determined to find out. With every step she took, the air seemed to be charged with otherworldly energy, and Maple had the strange feeling that something important was about to happen.

Chapter 8: The Fairy Forest

Upon entering the Fairy Forest, Maple felt as if an invisible hand was guiding her along intertwined paths. It was almost as if she was walking through a magical portal into another dimension. As she walked, impelled by that invisible force, she heard the soft rustling of twigs and leaves on the ground, saw the dappled light filtered through the tall trees, and listened to the sweet chirping of birds. Butterflies and moths delicately flapped their wings, small insects came and went in their busy lives, and lizards hurried in a natural ballet.

The sound of an owl perched on a high branch echoed through the forest, followed by the squawk of a crow, indicating that she had come to the right place. In a clearing in the woods, Maple saw something she had never seen before. A bush with white berries that glistened with an ethereal light.

She heard a whispering voice telling her, "Come a little closer."

Maple, captivated by the beauty of the berries, approached curiously. She grabbed one of the berries and watched it closely. It looked like a velvety little peach, perfectly white. An irresistible urge came over her, a sense of desire she couldn't explain. She knew that wild berries could be potentially poisonous, but the temptation was too strong.

Without further thought, Maple took a small bite of the berry and then threw it away. Although she had only tasted a small piece, the experience was intensely rewarding; the truth is that the berry tasted like any other berry. But Maple, who had a weakness for collecting plants, couldn't resist the temptation to take the seed home as a souvenir of her encounter in the mysterious Fairy Forest.

With the seed in her hand, Maple was excited and full of intrigue. What secret did those white berries hold? And what did this encounter in the enchanted forest mean? With her head full of questions, Maple prepared to return home, feeling that her life had taken an even more magical and mysterious turn.

Chapter 9: The Sea

When she got home, Pancake was eagerly waiting for her. Her eyes filled with tears as she saw her loyal companion, who offered her his pure love without the need for words. Maple was flooded with emotion as she caressed Pancake, wishing she knew everything he had to say.

Suddenly, Maple saw herself reflected in one of the many mirrors that decorated her apartment. Her reflection in the mirror seemed to speak to her. "You're the sky; you're the water," echoed in her mind. At that moment, the smart speaker in the kitchen activated the music of Sky Water, Maple's favorite band, filling the air with their ethereal sound.

The TV screensavers also seemed to reveal never-before-seen secrets, plunging Maple into a state of wonder and reflection. The song suddenly said, "If you love him, set him free." Maple took Pancake out for a walk to Marina Willows Park, specifically to a part of the park she affectionately called Serengeti because it reminded her of the views of the African plains from documentaries she watched as a child.

Upon arriving at this special place, Maple heard an inner voice repeating to her the words of the song: "If you love him, set him free." With pain in her soul, Maple unleashed Pancake's strap, gave him a gentle kiss, and said, "I will always love you. You are free." Pancake quickly disappeared among the rocks as he jumped like a frog, leaving Maple alone in the park.

Maple continued on her way alone, with her headphones on once more. The music began to speak to her in a code that only she could understand at the time. The signs were clear: the sea was calling her. Maple followed in the footsteps that the music revealed to her, trusting her intuition.

Finally, the music itself told her where to stop. Maple took off her headphones and found herself on a rock facing the majestic sea. The waves crashed hard against the shore; the sky was dyed purple, Maple's favorite color. Suddenly, she saw something that stunned her. It couldn't be real, but Maple knew this was more than just a hallucination. It was something immense, powerful, something she couldn't fully comprehend.

At that moment, Maple realized that her whole life had led her to that very moment in that very place.

Chapter 10: Maple, I'm Mister Universe

Maple still couldn't believe what she was witnessing. No matter how hard she tried to close her eyes, she couldn't take her eyes off this scene that looked like something out of a science fiction movie. In the background, majestic mountains with snow-capped peaks rose with a grandeur that defied human comprehension. But what really caught Maple's attention were colossal eyes that glowed softly but intensely in the distance.

A sense of lightness invaded Maple's body as if she was floating in a state of pure serenity. All her problems, pains, anxieties, and stress seemed to vanish before the magnificence of that supernatural panorama. Maple couldn't take her eyes off the colossal eyes that seemed to communicate with her on a deeper level than words.

Suddenly, a series of strange symbols began to flash in front of Maple's eyes. They looked like ancient extraterrestrial symbols dripped in pure gold, and a powerful yet gentle voice resounded in her mind, causing her body to buzz like a bee. The intriguing voice said, "Maple, I'm Mister Universe."

What happened next is now history. Maple now finds herself dealing with a new challenge: facing the present with all that she has learned and experienced on this extraordinary journey. Her thoughts are filled with questions and reflections as she immerses herself in this new chapter of her life.

Chapter 11: Snap out of it, Maple

Maple was lying in her bed with thoughts swirling around in her head. Could it be that she was really crazy, or was Mister Universe real? It all felt extremely real; many of the things that Maple had experienced in what the doctors wanted to call psychotic episodes were too astounding to be simple creations of Maple's brain. After all, neither the doctors nor anyone else had lived through everything Maple went through. No one in this life really understood her.

Maple was lost in a whirlwind of thoughts and memories of her experiences with Mister Universe when suddenly Bagel, her friend Julie's cat, whom Maple was taking care of, meowed in his trademark croaky tone, and Maple said to herself, I don't have time to go crazy, I have millions of followers who need me.

Maple got out of bed and went to the kitchen; as she passed through the hallway, she looked at herself in one of the mirrors and said to herself, I must not forget that my purpose in this life is special. I must never forget rule number one, as she looked at herself in the mirror, she saw one of her paintings that she had hanging on the opposite wall, and she turned to look at it. Maple admired the beauty of her abstract creation; the golden tones reminded her of those symbols that flashed in front of her eyes when she met Mister Universe. Maple said to herself, I have not painted anything new for a while; I should start painting again.

Maple went to the pantry and grabbed some plant-based cat treats and gave them to Bagel. Pancake's snores rumbled on the couch. Maple went and kissed him all over his body and spoke to him in silly voices. Pancake woke up happily. Maple decided she would go to the park, and this time, she would take both Pancake and Bagel; then she put the harness on Pancake and clipped the leash, then decided to look for the cat backpack with the clear plastic front. Julie had warned her that Bagel hated getting into that backpack and that if he saw it, he would hide.

Maple, believing herself to be smarter than Bagel, discreetly puts the backpack on the couch, ready to place Bagel in, and goes to the pantry to get more snacks to trick him into the backpack, but Bagel was more astute; he was already hiding. Maple called him and shook the container of cat treats, but Bagel would not come out of hiding.

Maple looked for him everywhere, under the bed, in the closet, in the laundry room, in the bathtub, literally everywhere. She was about to give up as she sat down on the couch to tie her shoelaces, already accepting the fact that she would have to go to the park just with Pancake, who was anxiously waiting, when suddenly, behind the TV, Maple sees Bagel's tail moving stealthily, Maple knows she has to be careful. She approaches quietly and forcibly catches him and puts him in his backpack. Bagel resists, but Maple's stubbornness is more than just determination. Maple wants to take him to the park, and she is going to take him to the park!

Finally, Maple succeeds; Bagel's face is suddenly serious but super comical. Maple feels a little sorry, but the scene is too funny; Maple knows that being a house cat, there are few opportunities for Bagel to explore the world, so with this goal achieved, Maple checks that she has everything in hand: keys, wallet, phone, and bag with water, wildflower seeds and food to feed the birds and small creatures of Marina Willows.

Maple was about to leave the apartment, when she remembered what Mister Universe had told her the last time she saw him, and she grabbed her divination cards, which she had not used in a while, and she went out with Pancake and Bagel for the day's adventure at Marina Willows.

Chapter 12: The Everlasting Candle

As Maple walked towards Marina Willows with Bagel on her back and Pancake tugging at the leash, she decided to pause and pull out one of her divination cards. These cards, beautifully handcrafted by Maple, were mostly created before her first encounter with Mister Universe. To Maple, these cards came through a supernatural kind of inspiration, though she didn't know how or why she had created them.

In the last encounter with Mister Universe, he mentioned the cards, which stoked Maple's inner conflict between the supernatural and the rational. Maple wondered if it was best to completely forget about Mister Universe and everything she had experienced back then. Although many of the events had been erased from her memory, most were still alive in her mind.

Maple quickly tied Pancake to a bench near the park and took the cards out of the bag. She shuffled the cards quickly and pulled one out, which turned out to be a mysterious card: The Everlasting Candle. She had never drawn this card before, though she remembered crafting it.

For a moment, Maple wondered if the card had any special meaning, but she said to herself, "Maple, don't be silly. The cards are as crazy as you are." She put the card back in her backpack, untied Pancake, and continued toward the park, trying to push the unsettling doubts and thoughts out of her mind.

Chapter 13: Good Luck

Bagel began to meow from inside the backpack while Pancake circled around Maple. Maple normally expected to get to the part of the park where the other dogs ran free to remove Pancake's leash, but since they were with Bagel, she decided to release him in the Serengeti, near the same place where she had let him go that time before seeing Mister Universe's eyes. But this time, she wouldn't let him go.

Maple continued to walk with Bagel on her back and Pancake running free at a close distance. Suddenly, Maple saw a peacock courting a peahen, plumage in full bloom while performing a mesmerizing dance. Maple knew what she had to do. She strapped Pancake up again, pulled out her cell phone and sneaked up to start recording a live broadcast for her millions of followers.

Maple's videos, often simple samples of the beauty of nature, had managed to captivate an exorbitant number of followers, who appreciated the beauty of Earth through their phones. As the peacock danced captivatingly, Maple reminded her followers of her number one rule: "Don't forget rule number one." On the cell phone screen, hundreds of hearts, and then thousands, began to appear. Maple stopped the transmission and set about walking with the dog and cat.

Suddenly, Maple saw a man who appeared to be homeless, surrounded by crows. Maple decided to record the interaction between this man and the crows. She had had a special relationship with crows during her "episodes." She watched and recorded for a while before stopping the recording. Maple felt the need to help those most in need.

She walked up to the man and greeted him. The man turned around in surprise and said, "Maple, I'll never forget what you did for me." Maple did not remember the man and asked if they knew each other. The man, amazed by the presence of Pancake and Bagel, began to tell her his story. Maple listened intently and, in the end, offered him some money to help him. Although the man was reluctant at first, Maple insisted that he accept it. She took out her wallet, had about $400 in cash, and gave it to the man, who insisted on not accepting it, but Maple told him, I have much more money than I need, accept the small gift, and if you really don't want it, help a friend or if you want, even a stranger.

The man took the money gratefully, and Maple, Pancake and Bagel continued on their way, leaving the man surrounded by crows behind.

Chapter 14: The Duck Lagoon

As Maple arrived at Duck Lagoon, a herd of geese began to run in her direction. They looked like they could smell the food Maple was carrying in the bag. Most of the people at the park were afraid of geese, but Maple perceived them as gentle and magnificent.

She decided to put the backpack carrying Bagel facing forward so he could see everything. Meanwhile, the presence of Pancake didn't seem to discourage the geese, and the presence of the geese didn't seem to disturb Pancake either, who just wanted to play.

Bagel's face inside the backpack was a mixture of "I hate being in this prison" and "Who are these individuals? I want to meet them." Maple took the bird seed out of her bag, and suddenly, not only the geese were chasing her, but all the ducks, crows, gulls, and even great blue herons joined the scene.

Maple's eyes were suddenly staring at the water; inside the lagoon, three turtles were balancing on a floating log. Suddenly, Maple heard a voice in her head. It wasn't her own voice, nor Mister Universe's. A delightful feminine voice said, "Hello, Maple. We have not been formally introduced. My name is Haja."

Chapter 15: Haja's Call

Maple fainted suddenly, but luckily, Bagel, who was on fer front, avoided any damage. People in the park ran to Maple to help her, but she remained unconscious. When she finally opened her eyes, she realized that she was no longer in Marina Willows, or at least not in the Duck Lagoon.

She was in a place that seemed to be taken from a dream, a virgin world where nature exhibited all its majesty. A triple rainbow decorated the sky, while flowers of every imaginable color and shape adorned the ground. Crystal-clear waterfalls shimmered in the sun, forming a dazzling spectacle.

Animals of all species coexisted in harmony, creating a scene of peace and tranquillity. Lions rested next to zebras, crocodiles shared space with elephants, and in the distance, enormous creatures reminiscent of dinosaurs covered in colorful feathers moved gracefully. Caves filled with multicolored gems and an ocean of turquoise waters. If there was such a thing as a paradise, this must have been it, but there were no humans.

Maple felt as if she was floating, with no control over her own body, simply admiring the beauty around her. Suddenly, everything went black, and a voice echoed in her mind.

"Maple, I'm sick, and I need your help now more than ever. You have to go back to Haja Island. Look inside your pocket," Haja's voice said.

Maple opened her eyes again and found herself surrounded by people and an ambulance. Pancake and Bagel were with some sort of officer. The dream world she had been in seemed as real as life itself. What did this strange call from Haja mean? Maple felt more confused than ever.

Chapter 16: 1984

Maple was inside the ambulance, surrounded by the smell of disinfectant and the repetitive sound of medical equipment. As the vehicle moved through the city streets, Maple sank into her thoughts.

The year 1984 had a special meaning for her. Not only was it the title of a famous dystopian novel, but it also marked a spiraling point in her life. It was the year she was born, a time that was etched in her memory as the beginning of her existence in this chaotic world.

But for Maple, 1984 also symbolized something more personal. It was the year her parents, Pearl and Roman, settled their differences with the birth of their first daughter. Although their parents' relationship wouldn't last forever, at least at that time, they were a happy family.

Maple didn't understand why suddenly, after Haja's strange call, she was thinking about the year she was born. She began to reflect on what Haja had told her, that she was sick and needed help. Then, she remembered to look inside her pocket, and inside, she found a seed. But it wasn't just any seed; it was that little white berry that looked like a velvety peach, the same one she'd taken from the Fairy Forest in Marina Willows years ago before she met Mister Universe.

This revelation filled Maple with a sense of wonder and confusion. What connection did this seed have with Haja's call? And why had the memory of her birth in 1984 suddenly resurfaced in her mind? As she reflected on all this, Maple realized that the year 1984 represented a crossroads not only for her but for the entire world. It was a reminder of the challenges facing human societies but also of the resilience and hope that had always been present, even in the darkest of times.

35

Chapter 17: Sisters

Maple arrived at the hospital, and when she entered, her sister Honey was already there waiting for her. Before they could talk, Maple had to undergo some medical tests. After a brief time, doctors discharged her.

Honey approached Maple with a worried look and asked, "What happened?" Maple, undecided about whether to trust her sister, decided to tell a harmless lie and said that she had forgotten to drink water, which led to her dehydration.

Honey expressed her relief for Maple's well-being and then mentioned that they needed to talk about something important. The two of them went out together to Honey's car, where they could talk more privately. Once inside the car, Honey decided to be direct with Maple.

"Maple, I confirmed an appointment with Dr. Goldbucket, and I also spoke with Julie, who arrives tonight from Portugal. We believe that in addition to that, it is necessary to visit the psychiatrist to review the dosage and effectiveness of your current treatment," Honey said, worried.

In the face of this revelation, Maple remained silent. Honey continued, expressing her concern, "Are you still taking your pills?" Maple remained silent, unable to respond immediately. Honey looked at her compassionately and said, "Maple, I know I'm not always the nicest to you, but trust me, I just want the best for you. You are my sister and I love you."

These words touched Maple's heart in an unexpected way. With a solitary tear running down her cheek, Maple hugged Honey tightly. In the back seat, Bagel began to meow and Pancake to howl as if they could feel the emotional tension in the air. At that moment, Maple realized how important her family's support was in challenging times like this.

Chapter 18: The Seed in the Pocket

Honey took Maple to her apartment, where she was finally able to feel in a familiar and comforting environment. Upon entering, Maple observed how all of her plants were illuminated by the grow lamps, filling the space with a sense of life and vitality. Maple pulled Bagel out of the backpack and freed Pancake from his leash, allowing them to freely explore the space. Then, she served food to both of them and watched them eagerly devour it.

After making sure her pets were taken care of, Maple filled a pitcher with water and proceeded to water her many plants, devoting a little love and care to them. As she did so, a memory of that perfect world Haja showed her invaded her mind, and Maple wondered who Haja really was.

Haja's name was not unfamiliar to Maple. She remembered that one of her divination cards was called "Mother Haja," inspired by a painted rock that Maple had found in the past. This rock had helped her reach Haja Island during one of her psychotic episodes. Maple had visited the island daily, bringing with her seeds, soil, offerings, and even art, but when she began her antipsychotic treatment, she lost interest in the island and never visited it again.

Now, with Haja's voice urging her to return, Maple was at a crossroads. She wasn't sure she'd be ready to face those memories and emotions again, but feeling the seed in her pocket, Maple thought this couldn't be a mere coincidence. She knew she had to return to Haja Island.

Chapter 19: Lifeline

Maple's phone started ringing, showing Julie on the screen. Maple replied with a smile, "Hi Julie, how are you? Are you home yet?"

Julie replied, her voice somewhat tired but full of enthusiasm: "Friend, I just landed home! I'm super tired from the flight, but I wanted you to know that I'm already here and that you're not alone."

Maple felt a glimmer of relief as she heard her friend's voice. "Thanks for calling me, Julie. It means a lot to me. Do you have anything planned for tomorrow?"

Julie replied, "Yes, some things to do in the morning, but in the evening, we can have a girls' night, just you and me. However, if you feel comfortable, I can tell Honey."

Maple considered the proposal for a few seconds. "You can invite Honey. Honestly, I've been thinking a lot, and I think I must vent to you. I don't know if I can reveal absolutely everything that's going on, but I can share with you a little bit of what I'm experiencing."

Julie nodded sympathetically, conveying her support over the phone. "Maple, I've had my own weird incidents too. I don't know if my experiences have been as extraordinary as yours, but we can talk about it tomorrow."

Maple was comforted by Julie's words. "Thank you, Julie. It means a lot to me to know that I can count on you. Let's talk tomorrow, then."

Promising to talk more thoroughly the next day, Maple hung up the phone, feeling relieved to have Julie and even her sister Honey by her side in this difficult situation.

40

Chapter 20: The Summon

It was late at night, and Maple was exhausted. After giving Pancake and feline guest Bagel some snacks, she headed to her room. She got everything ready to go to sleep, and brushed her teeth, and as she did so, her reflection in the bathroom mirror spoke to her again. It was her own voice, but it seemed to be another soul speaking to her.

The voice said, "Hello Maple, Mister Universe has summoned you. He's waiting for you in that place where you called your dad that time."

Maple knew exactly where the voice was referring. It was "Cuervo Hills," that place inside Marina Willows where crows congregate near the oaks with the twisted branches, in the area Maple referred to as The Serengeti. A few years ago, Maple made a call to her father, Roman, who was still alive, and they started talking about things that had happened when Maple was just a child, painful things. In the middle of the conversation, Maple felt as if a higher force began to communicate with her father through her, reciting a magnificently beautiful but peculiar poem to him. After that poem, Maple warned Roman that his days on earth were numbered, and a short time later, Roman effectively passed from this life.

For Maple, that call with her father was one of the most special experiences of her life. Now, she wondered why her reflection in the bathroom wanted her to go to that place again. Although Maple doubted the voice, she felt an odd temptation to return to that spot in

Cuervo Hills. What did this call to her father really mean? What secrets or revelations awaited her there this time?

As she struggled between uncertainty and curiosity, Maple decided not to ignore the voice inside her. After all, she had learned to trust her instincts over the years, even when logic seemed to contradict them.

Maple looked at the mirror again and said, "Maple, don't let madness win. You'd better go to sleep."

When Maple came out of the bathroom to her bed, both Pancake and Bagel were on top of the bed waiting for her. Maple went to bed, but before going to sleep, she put on a hypnotherapy session to lose weight. Although she wasn't big, Maple was a little overweight, something she was always worried about. Her weight fluctuated from time to time, and it had always been something that troubled her, especially since obesity ran in her family.

Maple put on her headphones and began the hypnotherapy session.

Chapter 21: The Morning Meow

Bagel's hoarse meows woke Maple up at 6:12 a.m., as he did almost every morning. Maple, somewhere between sleepy and accepting, resisted for a moment to leave the warm embrace of the sheets, but she knew that if she didn't get up, Bagel wouldn't stop meowing.

With a sigh, Maple slowly sat up and slipped out of bed. Although waking up early wasn't exactly her favorite activity, the night's hypnotherapy session seemed to have injected her with an unexpected dose of energy, and now she felt determined to make the most of it.

After brushing her teeth in the bathroom, with Bagel prowling around her, meowing relentlessly, Maple made her way to the kitchen. As she prepared breakfast for Bagel and Pancake, she waved to her reflection in the hallway mirror, and she said, "Hi, Maple." Although she felt a little sleepy, a smile came to her lips as she remembered the renewed energy that swept over her.

After serving the plant-based cat food for Bagel and some dog food for Pancake, Maple prepared to take her pets to the park. This time, however, she decided to be more cunning and grab Bagel before taking out the backpack. The annoyed expression on the feline's face was so funny that Maple couldn't help but laugh.

With Bagel in his backpack, Pancake, and a bag full of stuff, Maple left her apartment and headed for Marina Willows Park. The sun was just beginning to peek over the horizon, and the crisp morning air filled her lungs, awakening all her senses. Maple knew that the day promised exciting adventures, and she was bursting with all the energy the hypnotherapy session had given her the night before.

Chapter 22: The Unexpected

Maple was heading towards Marina Willows with Pancake and Bagel, enjoying the leisurely morning walk before arriving at the park. However, before she could fully immerse herself in her thoughts, she heard her name. "Maple!"

As she turned, she was met by a man dressed in jeans and a Tshirt. Maple recognized him instantly. "It's you! You were at Marina Willows a few days ago, but you look completely different. Your hair is short and tidy, your clothes are clean, and you smell great. I'm sorry, I didn't mean..."

The man interrupted her with a loud laugh. "Don't worry," he said with a smile. "I know it's true. I didn't smell great and I was dirty, but to be honest, I was hoping to find you."

Maple was a little taken aback by the comment but waited for the man to continue.

"After our meeting, I decided to make some changes in my life," the man continued. "I wanted to thank you for your gift. It's been a while since I've cut my hair, and I said to myself, why not? Seeing myself in the mirror with my dirty clothes, I decided to take it a step further and went to the mall to buy a new outfit. That's when I saw myself reflected in the mirror and saw that me from a few years ago before alcohol became my constant companion."

Maple listened intently, her heart full of mixed emotions.
"Since that day, I haven't had a drop," the man continued proudly. "I decided to amend my life and signed up for an alcohol program

offered by the city for free. I also signed up for an employment program through an agency, and my fingers are crossed. But I wanted to tell you that, with the money I had left over, I bought food for several of my homeless friends."

Maple felt a lump in her throat as she heard the man's words. She couldn't believe the impact her small gesture had had on someone else's life. It was a powerful reminder of how even the simplest actions could make a meaningful difference in the lives of others.

Chapter 23: Animals Are Not Food

Maple approached the man, moved by his story and determined to offer her help. "I know you can do it. Do you need more money?" She asked politely.

The man pondered for a moment before answering. "Actually, yes, but I think it's time for me to take responsibility for my actions, and you should help someone else since you changed my life forever."

Maple smiled at his determination, and she thought of the card she drew the other day, "The everlasting candle," and how the flame of hope always stays alive. Then she said, "You never told me your name."

"Gaston," the man replied. "My mother used to say it was a name of kings."

Maple nodded, impressed by his story. "Nice to see you, Gaston. Don't hesitate to say hello if we meet again. I hope things continue to go well for you."

However, before Maple could continue on her way, Gaston stopped her. "Wait, I've got something for you. It's not much, but it means a lot to me."

He handed her a rock painted with beautiful, meticulous designs of flowers and animals. Maple looked at it charmingly and turned it over to discover a message: "Animals are not food."

Maple recognized the rock instantly and asked in surprise, "Where did you get this rock?"

Gaston explained, "I found it in the park a few years ago, and it opened my eyes. I had a cat that I loved more than my life, and I had lost him the year before my whole life spiraled into the void." Maple felt a surge of emotions as she thanked the man.

After saying goodbye, Maple looked at the rock once more, marveling at the chance that it returned to her hands. That rock had been painted by herself during one of her "psychotic episodes."

Maple was deeply moved by the encounter and by the message that life had given her. She continued on her way with Pancake and Bagel by her side.

Chapter 24: Choices

As Maple made her way into the tranquil Marina Willows Park, the man's words echoed in her mind like a persistent mantra. She paused under the shade of a majestic oak tree with crooked branches and let her thoughts wander freely.

For Maple, the decision not to consume meat had been more than just a dietary choice, but a conviction rooted in her deep respect and love for animal life. She looked around, admiring the beauty of the nature around her, and felt connected to every living thing, from the birds in flight to the little bugs about their business.

She recalled the words of Dr. Goldbucket, her therapist, and her best friend Julie's mother, who had taught her that the first step toward change was recognizing the need for transformation and that the first step was often the most difficult. Maple understood that challenging cultural norms and questioning entrenched practices was a difficult but necessary path.

With each step she took in the park, Maple reflected on the impact of her choices on the world around her. She knew that her commitment to an ethical and sustainable lifestyle was just the beginning, but she also understood that every small gesture, every conscious choice, had a cumulative effect.

The card of the everlasting candle she had drawn out of her divination deck also echoed in her mind. It was a reminder of the light that burns within each of us, a light that guides the way to compassion and wisdom. Maple was comforted by the certainty that she was on the right path, following the light of her own conscience.

As Maple walked surrounded by natural beauty, she felt renewed in her commitment to living in harmony with the world around her. With each sunrise, a new opportunity arose to be a voice for those who can't speak and an advocate for those who can't defend themselves.

With the everlasting candle shining in her heart, Maple continued on her way through the park with the firm conviction that animals are not food.

Chapter 25: The Pearl

Maple had inadvertently arrived at Cuervo Hills, the place where the voice in her mirror had summoned her. As she approached the spot where she had made that call to her late father, Roman, the crows fluttered restlessly. Pancake was a little startled, but Bagel seemed unfazed by the birds' agitation.

Maple stopped at the exact spot where she had been a long time ago, in a moment filled with memories and emotions. Suddenly, her phone rings, and it's Julie Goldbucket. Maple, surprised by the coincidence, answers and greets her friend enthusiastically. Julie, curious, asks if Maple managed to get Bagel into the backpack, expressing her surprise. She then tells her that one of the reasons she returned from her trip so abruptly was not only out of concern for her but also because she sorely missed her cat. Then, she informs her about the appointment with her mother for the next day and offers to accompany her if she feels more comfortable.

Maple is a little frustrated by the stigma surrounding her mental health but recognizes the importance of Julie's support. After all, Maple had heeded the reflection of a mirror. She accepts the offer of companionship for the appointment, and they agree to meet later for girls' night. As she hangs up, Maple notices a piece of mirror on the ground, reflecting a ray of light back into a Victorian-style birdhouse.

The birdhouse, built by Maple during one of her "episodes," was vandalized, and the roof was removed. Intrigued, Maple approaches and finds a sea pearl inside. She ponders its meaning and feels an instinctive impulse: she knows she must go to sea.

With the pearl in hand and a sense of determination, Maple sets out on her way to the ocean, following the call of Mister Universe and trusting that fate will guide her towards the revelation of new mysteries and truths.

Chapter 26: To the Sea

The sun was slowly rising above the horizon, tinting the sky warm and golden hues as Maple made her way down the path that led to the sea. Every step she took seemed to be accompanied by the symphony of nature: the soft murmur of the wind through the leaves of the trees, the melodious song of birds dancing in the air, and the intoxicating perfume of the wildflowers that lined the path.

Maple pauses for a moment to contemplate the beauty that surrounds her, feeling how the serenity of the surroundings invades her and calms her restless mind. Determined to share this experience with her followers, she pulls out her phone and starts recording with the camera in selfie mode.

"Hello, my beautiful little sugar cubes!" greets Maple with a beaming smile as she introduces herself to the camera. "I just wanted to show you all how beautiful our world is."

Maple records the landscape full of flowers, bees, and birds, describing every detail with love and admiration. Hearts and supportive comments flood the screen as her fans excitedly tune in to witness this very special experience.

As she continues walking, her eyes fall on a deer grazing peacefully under the shade of a leafy tree. Maple approaches cautiously, feeling the excitement throb in her chest as she watches the majestic animal in this natural habitat.

The screen showing hundreds of hearts as she went live. Maple approaches the deer, and suddenly, the deer approaches her and looks at her with impressive intensity, straight into her eyes, the camera capturing everything. Maple walks over and pets the little deer, and the deer points to the sea with its head.

Maple bids farewell to her followers and hurries to the sea; she knew exactly where she had to go, that rock facing the sea where she saw the eyes of Mister Universe that first time. When she arrived at the precise spot, she looked up at the mountains and was greatly disappointed to see that the colossal glowing eyes of Mister Universe were not there.

Chapter 27: The Reunion

Maple was standing in front of the ocean, feeling a mixture of disappointment and confusion. She had thrown the pearl with all her might, almost as an act of frustration and desperation, but she never expected what happened next.

Mister Universe's colossal eyes opened in the mountains, shining with an intensity that left her paralyzed. It was as if the universe itself was looking at her through those gigantic cat's eyes.

"You're late," Mister Universe said seriously, snapping Maple out of her daze. She knew she was in the presence of a cosmic force beyond her comprehension.

Maple was feeling overwhelmed by Mister Universe's presence. "I'm sorry," she muttered. "I got distracted along the way."

Mister Universe didn't seem surprised by her answer. "Have you forgotten 10:25?" he asked, leaving Maple even more confused.

The 10:25 riddle echoed in Maple's mind, reminding her that there were still many mysteries to uncover on her journey with Mister Universe.

"Life is like that pearl you threw into the sea," Mister Universe continued, his voice echoing through the air. "It's beautiful, but it comes with pain."

Maple was frustrated and upset. "Why is there pain?" she asked, unable to contain her confusion.

Mister Universe calmly replied, "We are all connected, and we feel the pain of all other living beings. We are one. You are part of me, and I am part of you."

Although Mister Universe's words echoed in her mind, Maple wasn't sure whether to believe them. "The first time we met, you promised a life full of love and happiness," she said, recalling her first meeting with him. "But I haven't found the love of my life."

Mister Universe chuckled enigmatically. "All in due time," he replied. "Remember, the first time we met, you left without saying goodbye. But getting Pancake back was more important to you than the creator of the universe himself. That's why you were chosen."

Mister Universe's words echoed in Maple's mind, leaving her with more questions than answers. Although she still felt confused, a spark of hope ignited in her heart. Perhaps, in the vast and mysterious universe, there was still some magic in store for her.

Chapter 28: The Lunatic

Mister Universe closed his eyes, plunging Maple into an enigmatic silence that left her uneasy. As she tried to connect all the important elements in her head—Mister Universe, 10:25, rule number one, Marina Willows' Hidden Order, the fuzzy white berry that started it all, and even the importance of the three turtles on the floating log—Maple was overwhelmed by the amount of information and symbolism she was trying to process.

Suddenly, Pancake started barking and Bagel meowing as if they were trying to get Maple's attention. She understood that it was time to go home, especially since it was girls' night and Julie and Honey were coming to her place.

Before leaving, Maple decided to draw another divination card. To her surprise, it was the Lunatic. It was as if life, or Mister Universe, were mocking her, throwing ambiguous messages that defied her comprehension.

Maple put on her headphones and hurried to her apartment. Upon arriving, she freed Bagel and Pancake but realized she didn't have any food for girls' night. She hurried to the supermarket, her mind filled with confusing thoughts and unanswered questions.

When she arrived at the supermarket, headed toward the plant-based snacks, she saw the man that Mister Universe had revealed to her on their first meeting. His grey beard, his perfect hair, his face... Maple had never forgotten it. It had to be him.

The man was examining the regular non plant-based snacks, oblivious to the injustice experienced by "food" animals. Maple's heart sank as she realized that, despite her dreams, he was not the animal advocate she had hoped to find.

She grabbed several options of snacks, both sweet and savory, and headed to the fruit and vegetable aisle, trying to chase away the disappointment she felt inside. Although she hadn't found the man of her dreams, Maple knew that her commitment to her values and her fight for a fairer world for animals would remain unwavering.

Chapter 29: Immersion

Maple returned home with the snacks and hurried to get ready for girls' night. Though time was of the essence, Maple couldn't resist the temptation of a tub bath, complete with bubbles and all the luxury. Before diving in, she lit a scented candle and played Sky Water music on the smart speaker in the bathroom.

As she entered the tub, the ethereal music enveloped her, plunging her into a state of deep relaxation. Maple closed her eyes and drifted into the melody, feeling the tension leave her body.

However, relaxation took her to an unexpected place. Slowly, she submerged in the water and found herself in a desolate desert, covered with trash and plastic, with animal skeletons and a wind that brought only dust and a rotten smell. Although she floated above this strange world, her body didn't feel light; On the contrary, she felt a tightness in her chest.

Suddenly, she heard Haja's voice. "Maple, I've been waiting for you too, before Mister Universe even," the voice said. "Haja Island is waiting for you."

Before Maple could answer, something pulled her out of that place, and when she opened her eyes, she found her sister Honey, who had pulled her out of the water out of concern for her wellbeing.

Chapter 30: Crisis

Honey picked up her phone and called the emergency service when she realized Maple was in shock, unable to say a word. Confusion took hold of Honey, who panicked as she tried to understand what was happening. Suddenly, the doorbell rang, it was Julie, who had arrived early without knowing anything about what had happened.

Seeing Honey in a state of agitation, Julie asked what had happened, and Honey quickly took her to the bathroom, where they found Maple still in shock. Just then, the doorbell rang again; it was the police.

Honey led the two officers to the bathroom, where Maple was covered with a towel while Julie was trying to help her. Honey explained the situation, but the cops insisted that Maple had tried to harm herself, and they had to take her to the psychiatric hospital.

The situation became even more tense when the cops decided to handcuff Maple to "prevent her from harming herself or others." Julie and Honey found themselves in shock and rage, but they knew they had no choice but to follow the police car to the mental hospital.

Chapter 31: Chaos

Upon arrival at the psychiatric hospital, Maple was injected with a tranquilizer and locked in a room. Suddenly, she began to speak in strange tongues, which alarmed the hospital staff. The nurses called the doctor, who took a few minutes to arrive.

When the doctor finally arrived, Maple was still talking nonsense and started screaming at the top of her lungs. Chaos engulfed the room as Maple became increasingly hostile, kicking and throwing punches as if defending herself from something invisible.

The doctor called two nurses to help her control Maple, and together, they managed to restrain her and tie her to the bed. Eventually, the effect of the tranquilizer began to take effect, and Maple fell asleep, exhausted from the struggle.

Closing her eyes, Maple found herself back in Cuervo Hills, where a mysterious woman with long hair and inverted feet appeared before her. The woman carried a torch that emitted an almost magical light, and her dog followed silently. Maple didn't know if the woman was coming or going away, but she felt a strange pull to her and a sense of mystery that enveloped her completely.

Chapter 32: Scarlett

The mysterious woman with long hair and inverted feet sang a melody that enveloped Maple in a deep trance. Was she Haja, the figure who had been haunting Maple's visions?

As the woman sang, the day melted into the night, and the light of the moon and the stars painted the waves of the sea. The woman's dance seemed to take her in opposite directions, confusing Maple as to whether she was approaching or moving away.

The trance led her to a well, similar to the one Maple had seen in her divination cards as "The Overflowing Well," the same well she had found in Haja Island a few years before. The woman approached the well and drank alongside her dog, who didn't make a single sound.

Maple tried to get closer to the well, but each step seemed to push her farther away. Suddenly, the woman turned to Maple and emitted a screech that scared away the nearby birds. As if by magic, she appeared right in front of Maple, and the name "Scarlett" resounded in her mind.

Maple understood that she wasn't Haja but someone else entirely. Scarlett was her own name, perhaps, but maybe it was a clue. Clarity enveloped her suddenly, and although she was aware that she was not on the earthly plane, she decided to awaken from that strange dream. Forcing her eyes open, she found herself tied to a bed in a psychiatric hospital room, screaming for help as nurses ignored her.

Chapter 33: I'm Not Bipolar

Minutes, hours, or days blurred in Maple's mind, and she felt as if she had been locked up for years. Suddenly, the doctor came into the room with two nurses and ordered her to be untied from her bed. Maple, puzzled, could hardly comprehend what was happening, but she felt a little bit of joy knowing that she would be released.

The doctor explained that she had been restrained to prevent her from harming herself or others and asked if she understood the situation. Maple nodded, but inside her, the whirlwind of emotions and thoughts overwhelmed her.

When the doctor questioned why she had tried to drown in the bathtub, Maple responded with a vague explanation about falling asleep during the bath. The doctor reviewed her medical file and reviewed the information about the psychotic episodes and the previous diagnosis of bipolar disorder. Then she says: "Your sister Honey told me some stories about your psychotic episodes a few years ago; I see in your file that the doctors at that time had diagnosed you as bipolar." Maple says: "I'm not bipolar; everything I lived was real, it's still real. I've seen Mister Universe again".

Maple adamantly rejected being bipolar and claimed that everything she had experienced was real, including her encounters with Mister Universe. The doctor took notes in her notebook and promised to arrange a call with her sister, Honey, or her mother.

After the doctor retreated and closed the door from the outside,

Maple was overcome with fury and the feeling of being trapped. A solitary tear escaped her eyes as her mind was torn between confusion and despair.

As she pondered her situation, her mind returned to the mysterious apparition in her vision. Who was Scarlett, and what did her presence mean in all of this? This question added to the 10:25 conundrum, creating an even more complex maze in Maple's mind.

Chapter 34: Freedom

Maple eventually got a call from Honey, but her hopes for freedom were crushed when Honey earnestly told her that her stay at the hospital was for her own good and that she would eventually understand. Although it hurt to hear those words, deep inside, Maple knew that her sister only wanted the best for her.

What Maple couldn't imagine was that the psychiatric hospital would become her home for a full month. During that time, Maple met other patients and bravely told them all of her experiences with Mister Universe, Scarlett, Haja, 10:25, and the overflowing well. To her surprise, instead of judging her, her fellow hospital patients marveled at her stories.

Maple made several friends during her time in the hospital, but one in particular, Katherine, made the time there more bearable. Katherine, affectionately called Katie, radiated a motherly aura that comforted Maple. Although Katie was discharged before Maple, they promised to meet outside the hospital.

During her stay, Maple immersed herself in reading books, had fascinating conversations with an elderly Palestine refugee, and played ping pong with her friend Mpule, who had recently arrived from Botswana and barely spoke at all but had the greatest and most authentic smile. Maple also engaged in creative pursuits such as drawing, crafting, and planting seeds that she saw germinate.

Finally, the long-awaited day arrived: Maple would be discharged from the hospital. With mixed emotions, she prepared to leave the place that, despite its hardships, had been her home for sometime.

Chapter 35: The Origami Whale

As Maple waited for Julie, who was coming to pick her up from the hospital, Mpule knocked on her bedroom door. In her best words, Mpule told Maple that she would miss her and handed her a small origami in the shape of a whale made from one of the pages of the mandala coloring book. Gratefully, Maple accepted the gift, being touched by the gesture of friendship.

Before Mpule left, Ashraf, the elderly Palestine refugee, also knocked on the door. He presented Maple with a book on Caribbean mythology, adorned with two photographs he had taken before his admission to the hospital. One of the images showed a tree, and the other was abstract in nature. Ashraf confessed to Maple that he had always dreamed of a vacation in the Greater Antilles and that he never lost hope of one day being able to visit them. Although Maple was at first hesitant to accept the book, Ashraf lovingly insisted.

Mpule proposed to play one last round of ping pong before Maple's release. Maple agreed, and they made their way to the floor's recreation room, with Ashraf following them to witness the game. As the game progressed, other patients congregated and began cheering. At the most exciting point of the game, the nurse called Maple to let her know it was time to leave. Distracted by the interruption, Maple lost the last point, leaving Mpule as the winner of the final game.

Despite the loss in the game, Maple said goodbye with a smile, grateful for the time spent with her friends at the hospital. She was ready to be outside of those walls. And most importantly, she couldn't wait to see her everything, Pancake. She grabbed a little pot with a few germinated flower seeds.

Chapter 36: Sweet Stop

Julie arrived at the hospital along with Honey, and Maple, seeing them, couldn't help but smile. She walked over quickly and hugged them tightly. Honey, usually reserved in her emotions, couldn't hold back tears at Maple's release. Julie and Honey bordered her with questions, eager to hear every detail of her hospital experience.

Maple, feeling the weight of her recent release, decided to be selective in her storytelling. She chose to skip the most distressing moments, choosing to focus on the small victories and human connections she had cultivated during her hospital stay.

Maple asked if they could walk to the house, the girls agreed, and Julie suggested that Honey take her car to Maple's apartment to prepare for her return. As they made their way through the familiar streets, Maple shared anecdotes from her days in the hospital, from the deep conversations with the other patients to the laughs shared during games.

At an impromptu stop at a gas station, Julie offered Maple the opportunity to pick out whatever she wanted from the store. Maple, her eyes shining with newfound freedom, explored the shelves and found gummy worms made from agar-agar and a mango-flavored aloe drink. It was a small indulgence, but for Maple, it meant more than just a sweet bite and a drink. It was a tangible reminder of her freedom and the sweetness of life outside the hospital walls.

With her loot in hand, Maple walked alongside Julie back home, savoring every step and bite as symbols of a new beginning filled with promise and hope.

Chapter 37: Welcome Home

Julie and Maple arrived home, and excitement erupted as Pancake and Bagel ran toward them, barking and wagging their tails with overflowing glee. Ria, Maple's roommate, came out of her room and hugged Maple affectionately, expressing her relief at seeing her back. Maple thanked Ria for taking care of Pancake while she was away, feeling deeply grateful for the care given to her beloved dog.

Honey approached Maple with a pharmacy bag in her hand, explaining that the doctors had changed her medication and increased the dose. Maple felt a surge of frustration at the prospect of adjusting to new medications, remembering how difficult the transition was last time and how those medications seemed to extinguish her life's spark. However, she accepted the bag with resignation, recognizing the importance of following the treatment.

Honey also informed Maple that they had moved the appointment with Dr. Dinorah Goldbucket, Julie's mother, to next Wednesday. Although Maple wasn't thrilled by the appointment, she understood the need to attend and not disappoint Honey and Julie. However, the prospect of facing Dr. Goldbucket did not fill her with joy.

Julie noticed the sadness in Maple's expression and offered her unconditional support on Wednesday. Maple was a little relieved to know she wouldn't be alone at the appointment. With the promise that Julie would be by her side, Maple began to feel a little more comfort in the face of the coming adversities.

Chapter 38: Farewells

Julie had left Bagel in Ria's care during the month Maple was in the hospital while renovation work was being done on her condo. However, the night before, the workers had finished their work, and Julie could finally bring her beloved Bagel back home. Julie had longed for that moment for the entire time she was separated from her faithful companion, deeply missing the warm hugs and shared moments.

For Maple, Bagel's departure was emotionally challenging. Although she was happy for Julie, who would finally be reunited with her beloved cat, Maple wasn't ready to say goodbye to Bagel. The little feline had brought unexpected joy into her life over the past month, being her constant companion in moments of solitude and silence. Although Maple took comfort in knowing that her loyal companion, Pancake, would still be by her side, Bagel's departure left a void in her heart.

With Julie and Bagel leaving together and Honey going her way, Maple found herself home alone with Pancake. Ria, as usual, was engrossed in her room, immersed in strategy games on her computer, or at least that's what Maple thought. Maple's mind felt clearer than usual, and the change in medication seemed to be working. However, a nagging worry still lingered in her head: she vividly remembered all the experiences she had lived, from the encounters with Mister Universe to the 10:25 enigma. The mystery remained unsolved, and Maple found herself increasingly obsessed with unraveling its meaning.

Chapter 39: I'm not crazy

Maple saw the bag of her new antipsychotic medications on the kitchen island. She examined them carefully and said with conviction to herself, "I don't need these pills. I'm not crazy. Plus, I feel perfectly normal." Maple took the container with the pills and threw them into a pot of plants, hiding them under the moss. Then, she spent some time pampering Pancake, reminding herself that, beyond any situation, he was part of her soul. Maple suddenly remembered she was an influencer with millions of followers who eagerly awaited her content. Maple had achieved a lot since she met Mister Universe a few years back; her life had taken a giant turn, and she had more money than she could have ever imagined, although she still rented a simple apartment in the center of the city with her roommate Ria, she didn't show off everything she had. She constantly donated to charity and the homeless, but the money kept pouring in.

She decided to check her social media, where the overwhelming number of messages and notifications reminded her of the magnitude of her influence. Although she always tried to read the comments, the virality of her content had made this task almost impossible. Maple thought of the video that had catapulted her to fame and searched for it, but for some reason, she couldn't watch it. Despite the accomplishments she had made since meeting Mister Universe, Maple felt that something was missing from her life: true love. A flash of excitement surged in her as she remembered the gray-bearded man Mister Universe had revealed to her in a vision years ago but then faded away. She knew it couldn't be him.

With a calmer mind, Maple reflected on her priorities. She needed a distraction from everything that was going on in her life, so she decided to upload a different video to social media. Just thinking about the creative process filled Maple with endorphins and excitement, bringing her to an elevated mood.

Chapter 40: Revelations

Maple grabbed her cell phone and opened her closet to pull out a tripod. She then proceeded to take out a canvas and a box of oil paints. She was going to do something she'd never done before: paint live for her followers. She set everything up, placed the cell phone fixed on the tripod, ready to record, and just before she started, her phone rang, and "Mom" appeared on the screen.

Surprised, Maple replied, "Hi Mom, how's everything going?" Pearl rarely called her. Pearl said, "Maple, I've been trying to communicate with you nonstop, and I've had no luck. Are you ok? Honey told me you're home." Maple confirmed she was fine at home. They talked about Maple's experience at the Hospital; Pearl expressed her happiness regarding Maple's release.

Suddenly, Pearl asked, "Does the name Scarlett ring a bell?" Maple was perplexed by the question. Maple asked why, and Pearl explained, "I was cleaning out your old room and found an old notebook from when you were a child. There was a very peculiar drawing of a woman with long hair and intense green eyes, but the strangest thing is that she had her feet inverted and underneath, you wrote Scarlett. I thought it was strange." Maple was stunned by this revelation and asked her mother to send her a photo on her phone. Pearl replied, "Of course, Honey." To which Maple jokingly said: "Mom, it's me, Maple."

Chapter 41: Connection

Pearl sends Maple a picture of the drawing and upon seeing it, Maple is even more stunned: It's the same woman she saw in her vision, the shaggy dog was also in the drawing, and she was even carrying a lit torch. How could this be? That drawing was more than 30 years old. Maple knew she needed to do more research, but she didn't know where to start.

Suddenly, she looks at the sprouted seeds she brought back from the hospital and remembers the seed of the velvety little white berry that started it all. She still had it in her pants' pocket. Maple grabs the seed and suddenly feels an energy take over her entire body.

Maple senses that Scarlett and Haja have some connection, but she doesn't know what that is. The only way to find the answers would be to return to Haja Island. But Maple hadn't visited in a while, and she couldn't remember how to get there. Maybe she needed help, but she didn't know who to trust. She didn't want to go back to the psychiatric hospital under any circumstances. She knew she had to proceed cautiously because, as Mister Universe had warned her, people weren't ready to understand.

Chapter 42: The Mirror

Maple felt like she was going through a whirlwind of emotions. Her mother's call, the discovery of Scarlett's drawing, and the mysterious voices echoing from her own head left her in a state of overwhelming confusion. What did it all mean? Was there something bigger at stake that she didn't yet understand?

She decided that she was in no condition to face her followers at the time. The need for answers overwhelmed her. She opted for a brief respite in the bathroom, seeking to calm her mind and find some clarity in the reflection in front of her.

Water ran down the faucet, filling the sink with a splashing sound. Maple wet her face, feeling the coolness of the water against her skin. She looked up at the mirror, finding her own reflection, but there was something different about it, something that disturbed her.

With a sigh, she turned to her reflection with a mixture of frustration and anxiety. "None of this makes any sense," Maple muttered, desperately searching for a rational explanation for everything that was happening.

To her surprise, the image in the mirror seemed to come to life for a moment, distorting slightly before taking on a more defined shape. The voice that came out of her was not hers; it was deep and resonant as if it came from somewhere beyond reality itself. It was the voice of Mister Universe himself.

"It all makes sense, but meaning is not linear," the voice echoed, sending shivers down Maple's spine. The gaze of her own reflection was piercing, it contained knowledge that transcended human understanding.

Maple gasped, unable to look away. What did it all mean? Was she going crazy, or was there something else at play? The voice in the mirror didn't give her direct answers; it just planted more questions in her already troubled mind.

Chapter 43: In Search of the Lost Signs

Maple understood that in order to understand everything, she had to try to make contact with Haja somehow, as Mister Universe apparently liked mind games and puzzles. Perhaps Haja was in the most obvious place, Haja Island, but the problem was that Maple couldn't remember how to get to Haja Island. When the screensaver of Maple's computer shows a picture of a turtle, suddenly an idea came to her mind; Maple remembered that when she saw the three turtles balancing on a floating log in the Duck Lagoon in Marina Willows Park, she had made contact with Haja. Maple gave Pancake a hug and a kiss and headed to the park alone.

Maple was in Marina Willows, a place full of memories and mysteries, hoping to find some clue that would lead her to Haja. The image of the three turtles on the floating log resonated in her mind as a key to unraveling the enigma surrounding the mysterious island.

With determination, Maple ventured into the park's Serengeti, leaving the trails behind and into familiar territory, Cuervo Hills. In the distance, she caught sight of the quaint Victorian-style birdhouse, a reminder of the beauty hidden in every corner of this place.

The memory of the pearl she had thrown into the sea came back to her, bringing with it the echo of Mister Universe's words: "Life is beautiful, but it comes with pain." Maple knew finding answers wouldn't be easy, but she was determined to keep going.

Following the trails adorned with yellow and white daffodils, Maple finally arrived at the Duck Lagoon, the place where she hoped to find the three turtles she was looking for. However, to her surprise, there was no sign of them.

Discouraged but not defeated, Maple decided to explore further. She watched ducks splashing in the water, geese squawking on the grass, and herons flying gracefully. Where could the turtles be?

Maple paused for a moment, closing her eyes and invoking in her mind the image of the three turtles balanced on the floating log. She was looking for a sign, a clue to guide her in her quest. Then, a slight movement on the surface of the water caught her attention. When she opened her eyes, she saw a small turtle timidly peeking out from among the bushes, followed by two others that followed close behind.

Maple's heart skipped a beat with excitement. She had found what she was looking for. With careful steps, she approached the lagoon, watching in wonder as the three turtles glided elegantly through the water. It was as if they were waiting for her arrival as if they knew she needed to find them.

Maple smiled, feeling a sense of renewed hope. She had found the signs she was looking for, and she knew that the turtles would guide her on her path to the truth. With determination in her heart, she set out to follow the path these beautiful creatures showed her, knowing that each step brought her one step closer to the mystery surrounding Haja and all the answers she so longed to find.

Chapter 44: Prisoner in Paradise

Maple watched intently as the turtles struggled to climb onto the floating log, feeling a strange connection to their effort to reach the goal. However, the scene became more and more discouraging as, one after another, they fell into the water as if trapped in a never-ending cycle of attempts and failures.

On the verge of giving up, Maple watched in amazement as the third turtle finally managed to climb onto the floating log. A wave of hope swept over her, but before she could react, she felt her consciousness fade, and she fell into a deep trance.

Upon awakening, she found herself in a cage in the middle of the paradise Haja had shown her earlier. Confused and alarmed, Maple desperately began to call out Haja's name but was greeted only by a dead silence.

The feeling of being trapped took hold of her, and Maple felt uncertainty and fear wrapped around her like a heavy blanket. What did it all mean? Why was she there? The questions echoed in her mind, but the answers seemed farther away than ever.

Determinedly, Maple decided not to panic. She took a deep breath and began to scan her surroundings, looking for any clues that might help her understand her situation. But as she explored her prison, she realized she was completely alone, with no sign of life around her beyond the lush plants and exotic animals that decked the landscape.

Despite her fear, Maple knew she had to stay calm and find a way to get out of there. Her fate was in her hands, and she was resolved to uncover the truth behind this whole mystery, even if it meant facing the greatest challenges she had ever known.

Chapter 45: The Cage

Maple was trapped in the cage, exploring every nook and cranny for a way out. However, there were no visible doors or bolts, and the bars seemed impenetrable. As she desperately tried to find a way out, she noticed a solitary flower in a corner of the cage. Maple looked at it and touched it, but nothing happened.

Frustrated and feeling increasingly powerless, Maple desperately searched for a solution. She tried to get her forearm between the bars, but the gaps were too narrow. Her elbows couldn't find room to escape.

She closed her eyes to find calm in the midst of the chaos. As she closed her eyes and immersed herself in her thoughts, a voice echoed in her mind, telling her that the bars in the cage were her own fears.

Opening her eyes, Maple saw that the bars had disappeared, making room for freedom. At that moment, Haja's voice called out again, revealing that she was suffering and needed Maple's help. She mentioned that the members of the Hidden Order were waiting for her in Marina Willows and left a glimmer of hope in Maple's heart.

Suddenly, the scene changed abruptly, and Maple found herself back in the hospital. Though confused by what she had just experienced, Maple felt a renewed sense of purpose. She knew she had to find out more about the hidden order and find a way to help Haja.

Chapter 46: An Unexpected Awakening

Opening her eyes in the hospital room, Maple is stunned to see her mother, Pearl, and her husband, Lars, asleep on a small couch near her bed. Pearl wakes up to notice that Maple is awake and gives her a warm welcome.

Maple, still bewildered, asked her mother how much time had passed. Pearl informs her with concern that it's been eight days since Maple fell into a coma. Maple can hardly believe it, feeling as if it was only a brief instant.

Before Pearl sets out to find a nurse, Lars wakes up with shock and joy to see Maple conscious. He expresses his relief and happiness to see her awake and well. Maple asks Lars if he's been painting, to which he replies that his inspiration has been off lately.

Maple, feeling identified, tells Lars about her own plans to paint. The conversation between them helps Maple feel a little more connected to reality and better understand the situation she finds herself in.

Chapter 47: In Search of Answers

After a series of medical tests, doctors determined that there was nothing serious with Maple, so she was discharged that same afternoon. Pearl and Lars accompanied her to her apartment, where Pancake greeted them with overflowing joy. Maple was happy to be home again, but she knew she had a lot to do.

In her mind, the number one priority was to get to Haja Island. Maple needed answers, and Haja had mentioned the Hidden Order in Marina Willows. Although Maple was already part of the order, she had lost contact and now had to find a way to get back. She knew that this connection was the key to returning to Haja Island.

Determined, Maple headed toward Marina Willows. Arriving at the park, she felt as if an invisible force was guiding her again. She followed paths that looked like labyrinths, circling in seemingly infinite circles. But suddenly, she heard voices in the distance, and she knew that she had arrived at the Hidden Order.

Chapter 48: The Albino Crow

Maple heard the voices but saw no one. Suddenly, a voice echoed in her mind: "Welcome back, Maple. The island of Haja awaits you. The island in the lake has missed you. To get there again, you must follow the albino crow, who will guide your way." Although Maple had never seen an albino crow, she knew she would find it in Cuervo Hills.

Another voice added, "Mister Universe has set everything up for you to arrive without any troubles." Then silence filled the air, and Maple headed toward Cuervo Hills, searching for the albino crow among the black crows flying through the sky.

Finally, she spotted the albino crow perched on a twisted branch high up in an oak tree. Maple whistled, and the crow took flight. Maple began to follow him, following crisscrossing paths that seemed familiar but strange at the same time.

After a while, she reached the lake, where Haja Island could be seen in the distance. On the shore, Maple found an abandoned purple kayak with a paddle. Maple knew there was no time to lose. Haja was waiting for her.

Chapter 49: Hello again, Haja Island

Maple, recalling her previous trips to Haja Island, knew that swimming long distances had been part of the journey, but this time, kayaking would make things easier. After inspecting the kayak and making sure it was in good shape, she began paddling in the direction of the island.

As she got closer, she noticed that the island looked deserted from a distance. Not a single tree was to be seen, a noticeable difference from the lush greenery and wild creatures she so vividly remembered. Upon reaching the shore, Maple decided to investigate. As she walked, she found a circular well made of stones. Instead of water, she found a tree with fruit that looked like bunches of small limes.

Maple picked up one of the fruits and studied it. After cracking it open with her teeth, she revealed a pinkish-orange flesh inside. Maple decided to give it a try, and at that moment, she heard Haja's voice saying, "I've been waiting for you."

Chapter 50: Haja's Revelation

Hearing Haja's intriguing voice, Maple felt as if a blanket of emotions was hugging her body. Haja said somberly:

"Listen, the clock is ticking. My cries are drowned in the sea; I exist alone on this altar. Plastic runs through my veins, my blood spills into the ground, and black smoke coats my lungs. The pain of the most innocent is reflected in my mirror. My diamonds are just ashes."

Then she said: "Mister Universe, in fact, created everything that exists, and I am the living essence of his dreams. I am the sea, I am the land, I am the air, I am the beating of every heart. I am your mother and your mother's mother. I am life itself, and the ego of humans has poisoned me from within."

Maple listened intently, absorbed by every word Haja uttered.

"There's a very crucial mission for you, Maple. If humans don't evolve, we'll all disappear. Mister Universe is good-natured, but he has a temper and little patience. Don't disobey him again," Haja firmly concluded.

Chapter 51: Maple's Choice

Upon hearing Haja's revelations, Maple understood that she had been chosen for a reason. She recalled Mister Universe's words about being careful what she said, as most people weren't ready to understand and that her sanity would be questioned. Maple knew she had the platform to make a real change, as she had demonstrated with Marina Willows Park.

Suddenly, Maple found the fuzzy white berry seed in her pocket. She wanted to understand everything, but neither Mister Universe nor Haja gave her direct answers. They had their puzzles and riddles that she had to decipher.

Maple, determined, threw the seed into the dusty ground. As it fell, thunder resounded, and it began to rain heavily. Maple ran to the purple kayak and paddled with all her might, feeling the rain soak her completely. Arriving at the shore, she walked through the park until she reached the building where her friend Julie lived, which was right across the park. After ringing the buzzer, Julie responded with surprise.

"Maple? What are you doing here? Are you ok? Come on up!" exclaimed Julie as she opened the door remotely. Maple decided to take the stairs and went up to the 16th floor, where Julie lived in a luxurious condo decorated with exquisite taste.

Chapter 52: It's all happening again

Maple was soaked from head to toe, and upon seeing her, Julie was immediately worried. She asked her to come close to the fireplace and went to get a towel while asking her what had happened to her and if she was okay. Despite the confusion she felt about everything she was experiencing, Maple knew that she had to act normally so as not to alarm Julie, but at the same time, she needed to vent.

They both sat down on the couch and at that moment, Bagel, Julie's cat, made his appearance, meowing in his characteristic hoarse tone as he climbed on top of Maple, who was overjoyed to see him again. Julie insisted on knowing what had happened to Maple, clearly worried. Maple was quiet for a moment, then asked, "Julie, be honest. Do you think I've lost my mind?"

Julie replied truthfully, "Maple, I know everything you've been through. I think your mind reacted that way because your past traumas were eager to come out and release you. No, I don't think you're crazy, and if you are a little crazy, I don't care. I love you just the same."

Maple was relieved to hear Julie's words and decided to share some of what she had experienced: "It's all happening again. I've made contact with Mister Universe again, and I've also met a sacred being named Haja. Both have made revelations to me, and I have been chosen to convey their message to the world."

Julie, surprised, tried to process the information. Suddenly, she remembered an event she had experienced some time ago and told Maple, "The spirit of my nana Minerva visited me and gave me a message that changed my life."

Chapter 53: 'Absolute Power Does Exist'

Maple, no doubt, didn't expect that response from Julie. Suddenly, she didn't feel as crazy and asked Julie about what her nana Minerva had told her. Julie hesitated for a second, still couldn't believe that she had revealed her secret to Maple. Then, cautiously, Julie shared her experience: "I was in bed, and suddenly, I saw a being watching me at the foot of the bed. Although perhaps I should have felt fear, I didn't. I told the being to come closer. I didn't have a clear picture of Nana Minerva in my mind since she died when I was very young, but I knew it was her. And what she told me shocked me and changed my life forever."

Maple was anxious to know what she had said and asked with interest. Julie responded, "She told me, 'Absolute power does exist.'" Maple wasn't sure she fully understood its meaning and asked Julie to explain. Julie continued, "When you feel like nothing makes sense and it seems like you've lost control of your destiny, remember those words." She then added, "That revelation was what made me end my pointless relationship with Sam, and it was also the reason I left my stressful job at the marketing agency."

Maple listened intently, pondering how to apply those words in her own life. Then, she decided to ask Julie if she believed in ghosts. Julie responded with a mixture of uncertainty and conviction: "I don't know, but I think it's a possibility. And who am I trying to fool? Yes, I definitely believe in ghosts ever since I saw my nana, Minerva. She was there; I saw her with my very own eyes. She spoke to me; I heard her with my very own ears. She grabbed my hand, and I felt her warmth with my very own skin."

Chapter 54: Gloom

Julie says to Maple: As you can see, I've also lived through events that I don't know how to explain. Nevertheless, I don't feel that I'm crazy; I do, however, believe that it would do you good to talk to my mom about it; I think she can give you a new perspective on all this. Julie's suggestion to talk to her mother, Dr. Goldbucket, about her experiences left her feeling both apprehensive and hopeful. She knew that Dr. Goldbucket's therapeutic approach did not leave much room for the supernatural, and the thought of being dismissed as "crazy" filled her with dread. But Julie's calmness and her offer to accompany her gave Maple a little courage.

As they said goodbye for the evening, Maple returned to her apartment, feeling a mixture of anticipation and anxiety. Pancake's excited welcome at the door helped calm her nerves. Ria was wearing headphones in the kitchen, preparing her typical noodles; Maple remembered the unanswered questions that fluttered in her mind.

After greeting Ria, Maple looked for Pancake's leash, intending to take him out for a walk to clear her mind. But as she left the building, she realized with a feeling of gloom that her keys had been left at home.

Panic began to grow inside Maple as she frantically searched for her keys in every single pocket; she called Ria in hopes that she could open the door for her and Pancake. But there was no answer to the phone or the buzzer.

Feeling a sense of desperation gripping her, Maple decided to ask Honey for help. Despite the late hour, she dialed her sister's number and explained the situation, asking if she and Pancake could come for a visit.

Honey, accustomed to Maple being strange but also worried about her big sister's mental health, says yes, but that they shouldn't take too long since she had work the next day.

Chapter 55: Ciguapa

Honey's apartment was a sea of white. Maple hadn't visited her sister's house in quite a while, and upon entering, she was met with minimalist décor that radiated calm. The predominance of white contrasted with the exuberant green of a beautiful Monstera Adansonii plant that stood out. Maple recognized this plant, as her mother Pearl had one just like it.

Maple couldn't help but be mesmerized by the plant, which seemed to bloom under Honey's loving care. Curious, Maple asked if the plant happened to have a name, and Honey replied with a smile that her name was Ciguapa. The name sounded peculiar, and Maple felt like she'd heard it before, but she found it charming and expressed her appreciation of the name. Honey felt like a proud mother.

After a brief chat, Honey showed the couch she had prepared for Maple, but before leaving, she asked her if she was still taking her medication. Maple, feeling uncomfortable, lied and claimed that she was. The response reassured Honey, who expressed her joy upon learning of Maple's appointment with Dr. Goldbucket the next day, accompanied by Julie.

Suddenly, Honey remembered that she had some of Maple's belongings in her possession and handed her a small bag with the book and photographs that her friend Ashraf had given her, along with the whale-shaped origami given to her by her friend Mpule.

Maple felt a surge of excitement at the sight of the gifts from her friends at the hospital and offered to lend Honey the book.

Honey had just finished her last book and had nothing to read, so she accepted the offer and said to Maple, "Why not lend it to me, and I'll give it back to you when I'm done." Both, tired, retired to rest, leaving behind the day full of questions and mysteries to immerse themselves in the dreams that the night had in store for them.

Chapter 56: The Mysterious Thomas Woodfire

Maple and Pancake were curled up on Honey's couch, but sleep was slipping away from Maple, whose mind was filled with thoughts about her experiences and anxiety about her upcoming appointment with Dr. Goldbucket. She decided to distract herself and glanced at some magazines on the coffee table. When she opened one of them, she was surprised: it was him, the man from the supermarket, the same one Mister Universe had revealed to her at their first meeting, with his gray beard and his impeccable hair.

The article talked about Thomas Woodfire, a man known for his philanthropic work in organizations dedicated to reforestation and beach cleanups, causes that Maple deeply supported. Shocked by the connection, Maple went to bed with the image of Mr. Woodfire hovering over her mind.

Early in the morning, Honey woke up to go to work to find Maple still asleep on the couch, a magazine in her hands. She quickly woke her up and reminded her of her appointment with Dr. Goldbucket, as well as mentioning her own meeting with Thomas Woodfire, the owner of the call center where she worked.

Maple, surprised, told Honey that she had seen him in the supermarket. Honey laughed hysterically and told her that a billionaire like Woodfire was unlikely to walk around a supermarket like an ordinary person. Maple said goodbye to Honey, who left for work and called Julie to pick her up to go to the appointment with Julie's mother, Dinorah Goldbucket.

Chapter 57: The Time Has Come

Maple received a call from Julie, who told her that she had already arrived to pick her up. Maple and Pancake left Honey's apartment and met in the parking lot. Maple climbed into Julie's car, where Maple's favorite band, Sky Water, was playing, filling her with joy as she listened to it. Julie said to her gently, "Maple, I want you to know that you shouldn't be afraid. Mom can be a little intimidating, but she's fantastic at her job. I actually believe seeing her is going to be a meaningful benefit to you." Before heading to the appointment, they made a quick stop at Maple's apartment to drop off Pancake. Once they made sure the lovely shaggy dog was comfortable at home, they continued on their way to Dr. Goldbucket's appointment.

Maple understood Julie's words, and she was determined to approach the appointment with an open mind. She knew she couldn't tell Dr. Goldbucket everything, but she was still determined to give her a general idea of what was going on to better understand her situation. Arriving at Dinorah's office, Maple and Julie took the elevator. Each floor, Maple felt her heart pound faster. The secretary informed them that the doctor was finishing a session with a patient but would be available shortly. She chatted briefly with Julie.

It took about 20 minutes before they could see the doctor, but everything was fine. Maple and Julie had arrived early for the appointment. In the waiting room, Julie got to play her favorite mobile game: Fruit Smasher. Maple watched Julie's game, and seeing the fruits being crushed by Julie's agile fingers, she couldn't help but think of the fuzzy white berry, and Mister Universe, Haja, Scarlett, 10:25, and all the other supernatural things she was experiencing came back to her mind. Suddenly, the voice of Dr. Goldbucket's secretary, Danisa, interrupted her thoughts and Julie's game, announcing that the doctor was ready to see them.

The doctor's last patient came out with a very confused expression on his face as if he was reflecting on his life's decisions. Maple asked herself what that patient's problem would be and if she was the "craziest" of Dinorah's patients. The doctor came out of her office and welcomed them, expressing her joy at seeing Maple again, and also greeted her daughter Julie, who was accompanying Maple, with a hug. The three of them went into her office.

Chapter 58: Take a Deep Breath

As they enter Dinorah's office, she invites them to make themselves comfortable. Julie chooses an elegant chair, while Maple settles into an extremely comfortable green chaise longue next to a window that offers a panoramic view of the city and the beautiful Marina Willows National Park, Maple's favorite spot. On one side of the couch is a variegated rubber tree that seems to have grown too large for its pot. On the walls hang several professional diplomas and a poster with an image of the sea and snow-capped mountains, with the phrase "Take a Deep Breath" underneath, making Maple feel the almost mystical presence of "Mister Universe."

The doctor settles into her chair and begins recording the session, holding a sock puppet with red curly hair, eerily similar to Maple's. The doctor greets Maple and invites her to relax to the sound of the music, while asking her to view the puppet as a reflection of herself. Since Maple has been in previous sessions with Dr. Goldbucket, she is familiar with her peculiar method. The doctor announces that they are about to begin, closes the curtains and turns off the lights, leaving only a spotlight that illuminates the puppet, which seems to represent Maple herself.

The puppet turns to Maple, asking her who she is, and Maple responds with her name and describes herself as an artist and dreamer. The puppet continues to ask questions: "What are your dreams?" "What stands in the way of your happiness?" Maple says her greatest dream is to be happy; then she says, "Mister Universe says that I'm the only one who stands in the way of my own happiness," which triggers a series of questions from the puppet about who that being is: "What's been going on in Maple's life recently?", "Who is Mister Universe?"

Maple replies in a choked voice, "A lot has happened since I met him, Mister Universe; he is... It's complicated. He's like the creator of everything, but I don't know exactly." She recounted the story of how she met him years ago when she saw his colossal glowing eyes in the distance. When asked what stands in the way of her happiness, Maple pauses before answering, "I have everything anyone could want... Health, money, friends, but... My heart is alone."

The puppet continues to inquire, "What else has been going on in your life recently?" Maple hesitantly mentions, "Haja... she's been... in my thoughts."

Maple is comfortable sharing her thoughts and secrets with the puppet, even mentioning "The Hidden Order." The puppet goes on to ask, "Who is Haja?" "What is the Hidden Order?", "Have you seen Haja too?" "Is there any other being you want to tell me about?"

Maple, in a whisper, replies: "Haja... is... It's hard to explain. It's like the manifestation of nature... or something like that. I mean, I haven't seen her; I have only heard her voice." "There is also Scarlett, the woman with the backwards feet."

The session progresses quickly as the puppet continues to delve into Maple's thoughts and experiences. Finally, the lights come on, and Dr. Goldbucket takes back control of the appointment. In a more direct tone, the doctor confronts Maple about the nature of her beliefs, pointing out that "Mister Universe," "Haja," and even

"Scarlett" are figments of her imagination and questioning whether she has been following her antipsychotic treatment.

Maple, though a little disappointed by Dinorah's candor, falsely claims that she is taking her medications. The doctor schedules a new appointment for next week and says goodbye to Maple while staying alone with her daughter Julie for a moment. Maple waits at the front desk to leave, her thoughts all over the place.

Chapter 59: Doubt

Maple and Julie left Dr. Goldbucket's office and walked to Julie's car. On the way, Julie asked Maple how she was feeling after the appointment. Maple admitted that she expected Dinorah's reaction, but it still hurt her to think that she was really crazy. Julie tried to comfort her, suggesting that her mother just wanted to help Maple take charge of her mental health.

Julie made Maple reflect on the veracity of her experiences, telling Maple, "I don't think my mother ever said you're crazy. I think what she meant was that you're going through a somewhat complicated mental health process." Then, in a more serious tone, Julie continued, "Maple, think with a cool head for a moment. Do you really think you made contact with the creator of the universe and the mother of life and nature? Do you really think that's what happened?"

Maple felt a lump in her throat, first from the doctor's words and now from Julie's. Determinedly, Maple replied, "I know it's hard to believe, but I know everything I've been through. What's more, I can prove you everything. I'll take you to Haja Island." Maple determinedly stated that she was convinced of what she had experienced and was willing to prove it by taking her to Haja Island. Julie, however, was skeptical, noting that she had lived in the city all her life and had never heard of that island despite living across the street from Marina Willows. Maple mentioned the dry well with a tree and the fruits she ate as proof of the island's existence.

Although Julie felt a certain sadness at the thought that Maple might be delusional, she tried to cheer her up as a good friend. She proposed a girls' night at Maple's house with Honey, where they could relax, watch their favorite show, "Race for Fashion," and enjoy Carmenere wine to get away from the topics of Mister Universe, Haja, the Hidden Order and everything else. Maple, however, insisted that Haja Island existed and was determined to prove it.

Chapter 60: Rule Number One

While in her apartment, Maple decided to water her plants to calm her thoughts. However, she realized that they had already been watered. At that moment, Ria came out of her room with an empty plate of her typical noodle soups. Maple greeted her and asked if she had watered the plants, to which Ria replied in the affirmative. They talked a little about life, but Maple chose not to tell her anything about what she was experiencing, so as not to worry her. Suddenly, Maple told Ria that Julie and Honey were coming that night, and that she was also invited to share with them. Ria accepted and retired to her room.

Maple hadn't had her hypnotherapy sessions, which helped her change her eating habits, for a few days. Since she started the sessions, Maple had felt very little hunger, so she decided to resume them. Before taking a well-deserved nap along with Pancake, Maple put on her headphones and began to hear the voice inducing her into a trance. She fell asleep and suddenly heard Mister Universe's voice. She was trapped in that state, unable to open her eyes. At that moment, the last thing she wanted was to think about Mister Universe.

Mister Universe said, "Let's play. I've left you clues of the game everywhere." Maple asked what the game was all about, and Mister Universe replied, "If you want to understand everything, you can't forget rule number one." Maple had revered rule number one since Mister Universe revealed it to her years ago, but with everything going on, she'd forgotten about it. Mister Universe reminded her that rule number one was that she should have fun.

Maple thought about Mister Universe's game and how she could beat it. If she won the game, maybe he would leave her alone and allow her to be a normal person. But she admitted she loved rule number one. Mister Universe told her, "This is the most important game you'll ever play. You will understand everything, and by understanding it, you will have that total happiness that you crave so much." Suddenly, Mister Universe's voice fell silent, and the voice of the hypnotherapist returned, who told Maple that when he counted backwards from 5, she would wake up feeling satisfied and with a lot of energy. Maple woke up to Pancake licking her face, and suddenly the doorbell rang. It was night, and the girls had already arrived.

Chapter 61: Figure 10:25

Maple went to open the door and found Honey, who had arrived early. Honey told Maple that she had read the book she lent her and that it perplexed her. Maple hadn't read it yet and asked why. Honey opened the book to a page already marked, showing a picture with the figure 10:25 Ciguapa. It was a drawing of a woman with long hair, big eyes, but most shockingly: inverted feet. Upon seeing this image, Maple thought it must be the first clue of Mister Universe.

Suddenly, Maple asked Honey if that's what she told her that her solitary plant was called. Honey asked her to sit down and confessed to Maple that she had seen that woman, with her own eyes, not only in her dreams but also in Marina Willows. Seeing her in the book again sparked a whirlwind of emotions in Honey, who shared details of her own experience with madness. Maple couldn't believe the coincidence. Just then, Julie knocked on the door.

Honey told Maple that they needed to talk further about it, but later on, for now, it was better to try to enjoy girls' night. However, Maple was questioning her encounter with Scarlett, the "ciguapa", and couldn't stop thinking about one of the biggest enigmas of her entire adventure with Mister Universe: 10:25. She told herself that Honey was right, that she might as well try to enjoy girls' night.

Julie arrived with a bottle of wine and a packet of pistachios, greeted the girls, and they sat down on the couch ready to have a normal night.

Chapter 62: Race for Fashion

Girls' night had begun, and for a moment at least, Maple felt a bit of normalcy in her life. Honey and Julie were preparing the drinks and snacks while Maple knocked on Ria's door to invite her to join them. The four of them sat on the couch, and Maple excitedly put on her favorite show, "Race for Fashion," which was premiering its first episode of the season.

The competitors were from different countries this time, which excited the girls. With wine and appletinis in their glasses and pistachios and plant-based cheez crackers, they started watching their favorite show. Suddenly, ethereal music started playing, a song by the band Sky Water, which served as an intro to the tv show.

On the screen, images of people of all races wearing all kinds of clothes appeared, and sewing machines, rolls of fabric, needles, thread, and scissors flashed on the screen. A lonely catwalk appeared, and suddenly, the presenter came out: the famous pop singer "Gleeter."

She said, "Welcome to the eighth season of Race for Fashion. This season, we scoured the globe for the best fashion designers, but there's a twist: designers will have to bring their competitors' designs to life and not their own." They started introducing all the contestants, two from each continent, and suddenly, Gleeter announced this year's prize: "Half a million dollars!" The girls' jaws dropped in surprise.

Chapter 63: The Guest Judge

They had just announced this season's prize, a whopping $500,000. Ria, who didn't usually watch the show, asked, "How much money did they give out last season?" Maple and Julie replied in unison: "Half, $250,000." Honey, who had watched the previous season, told Ria, "This show is addictive, you're going to love it." Maple and Julie nodded, saying, "Absolutely."

The girls continued to watch the show, and suddenly, Gleeter thanked the sponsors, and the Woodfire Inc. logo appeared on the screen. Gleeter then introduced the season's judges: famous designers, models, and music artists. And as a special guest... none other than the CEO of Woodfire Inc., Thomas Woodfire himself. The four girls let out a collective sigh. Not only was Mr. Woodfire a successful billionaire, but he was also incredibly handsome.

Coincidentally, all the girls had something that connected them to Woodfire. He owned the old marketing agency where Julie used to work, he also owned the call center where Honey was a supervisor, and the library where Ria worked had been donated by him. But for Maple, Mr. Woodfire caused butterflies in her stomach and fire in her heart. Mister Universe had revealed his face to her years ago, though at the time, Maple had no idea who he was. He seemed to be the perfect man, but for Maple, there was a fundamental problem: Woodfire apparently didn't lead an animal conscious lifestyle, as she'd seen him at the grocery store buying some non-plant-based cookies.

Chapter 64: The Elimination

The girls continued to watch the show, eventually choosing the winner of the first episode, a girl from South Korea named Jaesoon. Then came the hardest part: elimination. In the background were two representatives, a girl named Altagracia from the Americas and a guy named Clive from Oceania. The girls were standing on end, waiting for the announcement of the eliminated contestant. The expectation was almost painful.

In her mind, Maple asked Mister Universe not to eliminate her favorite, Altagracia. For Maple, her design didn't deserve to be at the bottom; it was all Clive's fault; he had designed the original concept. All the girls were cheering for Altagracia. Suddenly, Clive's name is called, and Gleeter, in a somber voice, says, "The fashion race is too fast for you. I'm sorry, but you're going home."

The girls let out a scream so loud that Pancake, who was sleeping in one of his many beds, began to howl along with them. Suddenly, they showed scenes from the next episode, where designers would make fashion inspired by their continents. Honey said goodbye to the girls, as she had work the next day, and told Maple, "I'm glad to see you better; I love you," before leaving. Ria also said goodbye, going back to her room.

Julie was left alone with Maple, and they chatted a bit about the episode. Maple felt the need to tell her something important: "Thomas Woodfire, Mister Universe, revealed his face to me in a vision when we first met. I saw a life full of love and happiness."

Julie became even more concerned. She said to Maple worriedly, "Friend, I think Mister Universe is only hurting you in the end. If you want to be really happy, I think you should forget about him and start living a normal life again." Maple fell silent as Julie said goodbye, leaving Maple alone in thought.

Chapter 65: Whirlwind of Emotions

Maple lay down on the bed, but instead of finding peace, her mind was filled with turbulence. Thomas Woodfire's vision still haunted her, like a lingering specter that refused to go away.

She clearly remembered the image Mister Universe had shown her years ago: a life full of love and happiness, a life in which Woodfire played a prominent role. But now, with all she had discovered about him, that vision had become confusing and disturbing.

Julie's words echoed in her head: "Friend, I think Mister Universe is only hurting you in the end...". Maple wondered if her connection to Mister Universe had led her down a dangerous path if she had relied too heavily on the visions and revelations she had received.

The memory of the past few weeks swarmed through her mind, from her encounters with Mister Universe to the revelations about Woodfire and, of course, Haja. She felt trapped in a whirlwind of emotions, unable to find a clear way out.

On the one hand, there was the undeniable attraction she felt towards Woodfire, mixed with concern for his ethics and lifestyle. On the other hand, there was the mystery surrounding Mister Universe, Haja and the visions they had shared with her.

Maple tossed restlessly in bed, feeling the weight of uncertainty and confusion. Should I trust these visions, or should I leave them behind and seek a more "normal" life? And what does that really mean? These questions tormented her as she struggled to fall asleep amid the turmoil of thoughts.

Chapter 66: Finding Yourself

Maple decided to turn to her hypnotherapy session to find some peace and fall asleep. She closed her eyes and plunged into a state of relaxation, but instead of finding darkness, she found herself back on Haja Island.

This time, however, the island was unrecognizable. Not only was it deserted, but it was also polluted by trash and plastic covering the ground. Dead animal bones were strewn everywhere, and the tree inside the dry well looked like it had been cut down.

An ominous tick-tock echoed in the air, and suddenly, day turned to night and night to day. Heavy rain began to fall, clearing the island of pollution. The water washed away plastic and trash while the well filled up and poured with life.

Flowers, grass, and shrubs emerged from the earth. Giant trees soared into the sky, and hundreds of birds of all colors filled the skies. Insects, amphibians, and reptiles began to cross back and forth, creating a frenzy of activity.

In the midst of this transformation, Haja, the living manifestation of Mister Universe, appeared to Maple. "Maple," she said in a calm voice, "you have thrown the first seed, and the change has begun. Haja Island is eagerly waiting for you to find yourself."

Maple was overwhelmed by the magnitude of the moment. She had witnessed a renaissance on the island, a powerful reminder of nature's capacity for regeneration and renewal. She promised herself that she would further explore this mysterious place and seek answers about her own inner journey.

Chapter 67: Doris

Maple woke up in the morning with a sense of refreshment. Haja's message resounded in her mind, infusing her with new energy and determination. She decided to check her social media on her cell phone and discovered that her latest video had gone viral, something she was already used to.

As she was going through the notifications, she stumbled upon an important reminder: Today was her grandmother Doris' birthday. Without hesitation, Maple decided to call her on the phone. An elderly voice answered on the other end of the line, and Maple hurriedly congratulated her grandmother.

"Grammy, Happy Birthday! It's me, Maple," she said enthusiastically. But Doris's response took her by surprise. "Maple? Granddaughter? I don't have children," she muttered in uncertainty. Maple was puzzled for a moment, but then she remembered her grandmother's dementia and tried to explain who she was.

"Grandma, I'm Pearl's daughter, your eldest daughter," Maple explained patiently. But what Doris said next took her breath away. "Maple, I've been waiting for your call," she said with surprise in her voice. Maple was stunned. How could her grandmother have been waiting for her call if she didn't even recognize who she was?

Doris's response only added more mystery to the situation. "Mister Universe called me in my dream and told me to tell you that the clues were hidden in plain sight," Doris revealed, sending a shiver down Maple's spine. How could her grandmother know Mister Universe and mention him like that?

Before Maple could fully process what she had just heard, Doris added something else. "Ask your mother Pearl about Scarlett," she said enigmatically before abruptly saying goodbye.

Doris's words took Maple's breath away. Who was Scarlett, and what connection did she have with her mother? The mention of her name only added more intrigue to the growing list of mysteries surrounding her life. Maple knew she needed answers, and she knew exactly who to ask.

Chapter 68: The Overflowing Well

Maple didn't waste a second and immediately called her mother, Pearl. To her surprise, the one who answered was Pearl's husband, Lars, who greeted her warmly and asked if she had returned to painting. Maple shook her head, admitting that she hadn't found the time for it. Then, curious, she asked Lars if he had been painting lately.

"I got inspired!" exclaimed Lars enthusiastically. "I'll tell your mom to send you a picture of my last painting. I called it 'The Overflowing Well.'" Maple thought this was peculiar but didn't say anything about it. After a few moments of conversation, Lars said goodbye and handed the phone to Pearl.

Pearl greeted Maple warmly, but her tone quickly changed when Maple asked her a question that shook the foundations of her world. "Mom, who is Scarlett?" asked Maple in a trembling voice.

Pearl's response was visceral. Maple heard the sound of glass shattering on the floor, followed by a tense silence. "Daughter, it's a very painful story," Pearl began, visibly shaken. "Scarlett was my first child with Roman before you and Honey were born."

Maple felt a knot in her stomach as she listened to her mother reveal a long-kept family secret. "Scarlett was born with a congenital condition that appears to be common in our family for generations. She was born with her feet inverted," Pearl continued, her voice choked with tears.

The revelation left Maple stunned. Did she have another sister? What had happened to her? Why did they never mention her before? "Where does she live? How old is she?" asked Maple, unable to fully process the information she had just received.

Pearl, struggling to keep her composure, explained that Scarlett had passed away shortly after birth. Maple gasped at the tragic news. She tried to comfort her mother, assuring her that she loved her. Pearl was comforted by her daughter's words.

After a moment of silence, Maple promised her mother that they would talk later and said goodbye. The revelation about Scarlett left Maple with a mix of emotions: sadness over the loss of a sister she never knew, but also a renewed desire to discover more about her family and her history.

Chapter 69: The Silent Mirror

After closing the phone with her mother, Maple immersed herself in the intriguing legend of the Ciguapa, represented by the mysterious figure 10:25 in the book Ashraf had given her. According to legend, the Ciguapa was a nocturnal being that illuminated the nights with her torch and her magical entrancing melodies, protected against evil by a mute dog. Maple found it increasingly difficult to dismiss the coincidences as mere fantasies. She wondered if she was really experiencing bipolar disorder or if there was something deeper at play.

Determined to find answers, Maple headed to the bathroom to brush her teeth. Seeing her reflection in the mirror, she made a silent plea to Mister Universe, desperately wishing she was normal and happy. This time, the mirror remained silent, with no visions or answers. Maple felt a strange inner peace that she hadn't experienced in a long time.

She decided to take a breath and head to her favorite spot, Marina Willows, with Pancake by her side. As she prepared to leave, she noticed her deck of divination cards and decided to take a card to guide her way. To her surprise, the card she drew was that of Mother Haja, the central figure of her latest experiences. Maple couldn't help but laugh at the irony of the situation, wondering if she was really losing her mind.

With the card set aside, Maple and Pancake headed to the park. On the way, she heard her name being called: "Maple, Maple!" It was Gaston, the former vagabond with whom she had crossed paths before.

Chapter 70: Bicycle

Maple was overjoyed to see Gaston so transformed: well dressed, clean, and seemingly sober. She expressed her happiness at seeing him like this, and Gaston excitedly shared the good news: he had gotten a job at the Woodfire companies, a physically demanding job but with decent pay. Maple was surprised but pleased that things were looking up for him.

Suddenly, Gaston shared an even more startling revelation: his ex-wife had contacted him to reveal that they had a daughter he had no knowledge of. Maple listened with genuine happiness and curiosity, asking his daughter's name and age. With a smile, Gaston replied, "Her name is Scarlett; she's 8 years old." Maple was stunned by the coincidence of the name with the mysterious figure that had appeared in her life recently.

After wishing Gaston all the luck in the world, Maple and Pancake continued on their way to Marina Willows, with Scarlett's name swirling around in her mind. Suddenly, on a bicycle, she saw tycoon Thomas Woodfire pass by.

The chance of seeing Woodfire at that time and place seemed to charge the air with palpable expectation, as if fate were woven with invisible threads that connected them. Maple watched Woodfire's passage curiously, wondering what else fate would hold in her path intertwined with that of this powerful man.

Chapter 71: Puppet

Maple's heart was pounding when she saw Woodfire pedal his bike. Although she tried to deny it, the image of the humble and approachable tycoon only increased her attraction. However, her attention was suddenly diverted by a notification on her phone. It was a message from Pearl, and as she opened it, a photograph of Lars' last painting flooded the screen. Maple instantly recognized the well, the same well she had seen in her visions of Haja Island. This was a crucial clue, an unmistakable sign that something bigger was at play.

Maple's excitement intensified as she realized this could be her chance to prove to the world that she wasn't crazy. The coincidences were too many to be mere coincidences; There had to be something real behind all of this. Maple felt a sudden urgency to share it with the world, and without hesitation, she began recording a live message for her social media.

As she recited a poem that seemed to flow directly from the cosmos, Maple felt like a conduit for something bigger than herself. Were these her words, or were they Mister Universe's or Haja's, conveying a message to the world through her? Maple was perplexed by the magnitude of what she was experiencing, feeling that she was at the epicenter of a cosmic mystery that transcended her comprehension.

"In the vast expanse of the universe above, where stars twinkle, and planets move, Love permeates, a force so pure, Binding all, an eternal allure.

On this blue orb, we call our Earth, where oceans dance and flowers birth, rooted deep, like ancient trees, Seeds of hope, carried by the breeze.

In the cosmos, where mysteries unfold, Humanity's story, ancient and bold, Absolute power, a truth unseen, Guiding us through the vast machine.

Our emotions, like the ocean's tide, Ebbing, flowing, deep inside, yet clarity, a beacon bright, Guiding us through the darkest night.

Hearts beating with a rhythm true, Growth inevitable, for me and you, Connected, yet each one unique, in this cosmic dance, we seek.

Space, a canvas for energy to play, Nature's wisdom, in every way, Interconnected, yet fiercely free, in this grand design, we find our glee.

Amidst the shadows, be a guiding light, Happiness, our compass in the night, Animals, our kin, to cherish and defend, in their innocence, our love extend.

And amidst life's hustle, don't forget the fun, in plain sight, clues to be won, for abundance lies in every breath we take, in this grand adventure, let's not forsake."

Chapter 72: The Call of the Island

Maple's screen was filled with hearts reacting to her unforgettable, magically inspired poem. Suddenly, she felt as if she heard the voices of her ancestors in her head, each voice revealing secrets of existence to her. After watching Maple's live video, her sister Honey, clearly concerned about what she just saw, calls Maple.

"Maple, are you okay?" asks Honey. Maple suddenly says, "Honey, there's a party on Haja Island tonight; you can't miss it. Mister Universe and Haja will reveal their secrets to humanity."

Honey worries even more and says, "Maple, where are you? I'm going to you." Maple replies, "I'm going to Marina Willows' Hidden Lake; I'll be waiting for you." Maple shuts down the call with Honey, who panics and tries to call her back, but she doesn't answer. Honey calls Julie immediately, who tells her that she will pick her up to go find Maple.

When they arrive at Marina Willows, they use the GPS on their phones to find a lake with an island in the middle. It was a bit far away; they would have to pass through the Serengeti, through Cuervo Hills, until they reached the Duck Lagoon, through the Flower meadows and into the heart of Marina Willows. But Honey and Julie knew they had no time to waste; Maple appeared to be having a manic episode.

Chapter 73: The Call of the Stars

Maple begins walking towards Marina Willows' Hidden Lake, accompanied by Pancake. Arriving at the lake, Maple sits on the shore to wait for Honey, unaware that it has become dark. She communicates with the stars, which are just beginning to be seen in the heavens, and these, reveal even more secrets of existence.

Meanwhile, Julie and Honey desperately try to find the hidden lake. The GPS just carries them in circles, as if some greater force doesn't want them to arrive. When they lose hope, they hear a sound in the air: Maple's whistle. Maple used to whistle at crows in her online videos, and the melody of her whistles was indisputably Maple.

Honey and Julie follow the sound of the whistles until they find Maple lying in the grass, Pancake rolling around next to her. Maple is overjoyed to see them, and the girls are greatly relieved to see that Maple is okay. They say, "Maple, let's go home." Maple gets angry and says no, that tonight was the party on Haja Island and that they couldn't miss it.

Honey intelligently goes along and says, "Yes, we're definitely going to the party, but first, we have to go home to change our clothes." Maple thinks that sounds like a great idea, and they leave; while Maple talks about the interconnectedness of everything and how the party is going to be the greatest night ever for humanity, the party starts at 10:25 PM. Julie and Honey drive her to the mental hospital without telling her.

Upon arriving at the hospital, Maple feels betrayed.

Chapter 74: The Larger Plan

Before entering the hospital, Julie and Honey tell Maple, "This is for your own good and because we love you. Please, let's go voluntarily." Maple reluctantly agrees, but her heart is broken. Going back to the mental hospital was the last thing Maple wanted. It felt like she was taking a step back in her fight for normalcy.

Upon entering the hospital, Maple is taken to a patient waiting room. Julie and Honey wait anxiously in the main waiting room, feeling the weight of the decision they've made. They wonder if they did the right thing and if this is really the best way to help Maple. Their hearts are full of worry and doubt, but at the same time, they know that they are trying to do what's best for their friend and sister.

In the room where Maple is staying, the atmosphere is heavy and gloomy. The walls are adorned with murals of calm, comforting landscapes, but for Maple, they only add to her sense of confinement and hopelessness. She feels trapped in a nightmare from which she cannot wake up. Suddenly, Maple looks up at one of the murals containing a giant tree with birds perched on its branches, and it has abundant roots. This was a message from Haja, and it came at a time when she needed it most, a small spark of hope in the midst of the darkness that surrounded her.

Maple tries to decipher this message from Haja over and over again, trying to find her voice within herself and comfort in her words. Suddenly, she hears Haja's wonderful voice, and it reminds her that there is a greater force in the universe, a force that guides and protects her even in her darkest moments, that Mister Universe watches over her from the heavens and Haja on earth. Despite her heartbreak, a small part of Maple begins to cling to the idea that maybe, just maybe, this hospital experience is part of a larger plan, part of the path to healing and deeper understanding.

In the waiting room, Julie and Honey exchange worried looks. They wonder how Maple is doing and what she is feeling right now. Uncertainty and anxiety weigh on them as they wait for news of their friend and sister. They wonder if they will be able to help her find the path to the light at the end of this dark tunnel.

Chapter 75: You're Free

Suddenly, a nurse comes up to Maple and informs her that she's going to be injected with a tranquilizer. Maple, with little to do, lets herself get the shot and lies back in a relaxing chair while she waits for the doctors to see her. She plunges into a kind of trance as the drug begins to take effect.

Maple closes her eyes and finds herself in front of a giant tree, similar to the mural in the waiting room. She looks closely and sees a green parrot with a curved beak and white feathers on its forehead. The bird has shades of red, blue, and yellow on its wings and tail. The parrot begins to speak, repeating what appears to be its name: "Kooka, Kooka, Kooka." Maple follows her as she repeats the words.

The green parrot takes her on a magical flight to Haja Island again without the need to swim. Maple sees the overflowing well and walks up to it. The water flows endlessly, producing a magical sound and shimmering like golden glitter. Maple drinks from the water and hears Mister Universe's voice telling her, "You're free."

Opening her eyes, Maple finds herself back in the waiting room. She makes her way to an open door, unnoticed by the distracted nurse who is playing Fruit Smasher on her cell phone. Maple decides to return to Haja Island, feeling an inexplicable urgency to return to that place that seemed to hold the answers to her deepest questions.

Meanwhile, Julie and Honey become angry at the hospital staff upon realizing that Maple had run away. They decide to head to the hidden lake of Marina Willows, knowing that it is the place where they will find Maple. Concern and determination are reflected on their faces as they hurry towards the park. The night is increasingly darker.

133

Chapter 76: The Dance of Transformation

Maple arrives at the hidden lake in Marina Willows, expecting to see bright lights on Haja Island as a sign of the party she expects to find. However, darkness reigns supreme, and there is no sign of activity. Suddenly, she feels a single drop fall on her head, and upon coming into contact with it, she hears Haja's voice, who tells her that her actions have unleashed a wave of change and that joy is on the way.

Maple opens her eyes and finds herself in the pouring rain. Thunder and lightning light up the sky as the rain falls heavily. Maple understands that the celebration on Haja Island is no ordinary celebration; Haja is the venue, and Mister Universe is the DJ. Maple begins to dance with joy, feeling in her heart the certainty that a new beginning is on the way.

In her mind, she sees visions of a happy life with Pancake, with Woodfire's comforting presence at her side and the figure of a little girl filling their hearts with love, surrounded by nature's beauty. Maple gives herself completely to the music and the rhythm of the rain, feeling that she is in tune with the universe and her true purpose.

Suddenly, Honey and Julie arrive at the lake, soaking wet and with worried and panicked faces. They approach Maple and hug her tightly, expressing their relief at finding her safe and sound. The three of them head together towards Maple's house, leaving behind the night full of mystery and transformation, but with the certainty that they have experienced something extraordinary.

Chapter 77: The Dead Plant

When they arrive at Maple's apartment, Julie and Honey stay to keep her company. Julie notices something odd: one of Maple's plants is dead, which is surprising since Maple had always been very good at taking care of her plants, and all the others looked healthy and lush. Intrigued, Julie approaches the plant and carefully lifts the moss that covers the soil. What she discovers beneath the surface takes her breath away, and she discreetly calls Honey to see.

Honey examines the planter with a worried expression. What they find under the moss are several pills of an unknown drug. They decide that this matter is too serious to ignore and agree to contact Julie's mother to come see Maple the next day. For now, the most important thing is that Maple can sleep, so Honey offers to go to the pharmacy to get a syrup to help her fall asleep.

Maple, trusting her friend and her sister, takes the syrup they offer her. After a few minutes, she begins to feel the effects of the medication and eventually falls asleep. Julie and Honey, concerned about what they've discovered, quietly chat about the pills found and how they can help Maple deal with what appears to be a serious problem.

As Maple falls into a deep sleep, her mind travels back in time to Cuervo Hills, recalling a conversation with her father. At that pivotal moment, memories and emotions unfold that could shed light on the mysteries surrounding her life.

Chapter 78: The Last Call

Maple travels back in time to her last phone conversation with her father, Roman, shortly before he left this earthly plane. In the midst of her depression, Maple opens up to him, sharing traumatic events that occurred more than 30 years before when she was just a child. Through tears, Maple reveals everything to Roman, telling him what his cousin Darius had done. Roman, on the other end of the phone, cries inconsolably.

Suddenly, Maple feels compelled to recite a poem as if it were the culmination of years of pain and confusion:

"In a sea of dreams and hopes broken, an island lies in solitude, its essence lost. Divided by walls, separated by borders, the wind whispers an echo of sincere sorrow.

To the east, the light fades into cold shadows; to the west, the sun shines, but in empty souls. Two worlds in conflict, separated by destiny, two hearts longing for the same path.

But one day, fate changes course, and an invisible bridge is stretched deep in. The sea, a silent witness of this longed-for union, unites the shores in a dance of love.

The walls fall like leaves in autumn, and in each other's eyes, they find their seeds. The island, at last complete, shines in its fullness, united by the power of blossoming love.

Together, they walk along beaches of hope, weaving stories of peace with no more hate. A single island, united by an eternal bond, where love and unity are its rule."

Words flow from Maple like a cascade of revelations, as if each verse is a piece of the puzzle of her life that finally falls into place. In this poem, Maple finds a deep connection to her father, her own history and a renewed hope for the future.

Chapter 79: Morning Coffee

Maple wakes up, and it's morning. She feels excellent, clear minded, and lively. Getting up and heading into the living room to find Pancake, she finds Honey and Julie asleep on the couch, snoring softly. She tries not to wake them up but decides to make coffee to start the day. The aroma of coffee fills the room, and upon smelling it, Honey and Julie wake up.

"How are you feeling today, Maple?" asks Honey.

Maple smiles and replies, "Excellent, really. I feel really good today."

With a clear mind, Maple apologizes for worrying them and thanks them for their concern. Although Honey and Julie are still somewhat unsettled by what they found the night before, they feel calmer when they see Maple, more serene and at peace.

Before Julie and Honey leave, they inform Maple that Dr. Goldbucket will be visiting her and ask her to be on the lookout for her call. Honey sends a text message to Ria to keep an eye on Maple.

Maple is left home alone, and she decides to paint the painting she had planned to do live for her followers. She reaches for her instruments, sets up her camera, and just as she's about to start, the phone rings. The name Katie appears on the screen.

"Hello, Maple! How are you today?"

Maple smiles and replies, "Hi, Katie, it's been so long! I'm much better, thank you. I feel great today; how are you?"

Katie seemed relieved to hear that. "I'm glad to hear it. I was a little worried about you after watching that video you made live. I've been fine, I'm still on my medications, but I'm at peace."

Maple nods and apologizes for worrying Katie and the others. Then, excitedly, she tells Katie that she's about to paint live for her followers.

"That's great! Can I see?" asks Katie.

Maple nods and turns on the camera. She begins to paint with confidence and passion while Katie watches her admiringly from the screen. Maple is happy to have someone like Katie supporting her.

After a while, Maple finishes her work and proudly shows it to Katie through the camera. Katie is impressed by the creativity and beauty of the painting.

"It's unbelievable, Maple! You're really talented," Katie exclaims.

Maple smiles gratefully. "Thank you, Katie. It means a lot to me that you think that."

After saying goodbye to Katie, Maple is full of energy and excitement. She has found peace in her art and connection with the people around her. Now, she's prepared to tackle whatever life throws at her.

Chapter 80: What is the Truth?

Maple receives a call from Dr. Goldbucket, who tells her that she is only five minutes away. Maple tells her the number of her apartment's buzzer, 228, and waits for her arrival. When the doctor arrives, Maple remotely opens the door for her and greets her cordially. The doctor asks her how she is feeling and informs her that she is accompanied by a friend. Suddenly, she pulls a puppet from behind her back, that puppet strikingly similar to Maple. The doctor tells her to sit on the couch and relax.

The puppet asks if they can talk, to which Maple nods. Then, the puppet asks, "Who are you?"

"I am Maple Pelridge," Maple responds.

The puppet goes on to ask, "Who is Maple Pelridge?"

"Maple Pelridge is a child of the Earth and the Universe," Maple begins. "She's an artist and a dreamer."

The puppet then asks about Mister Universe. "Who is Mister Universe?"

"Mister Universe is the creator of everything that exists," Maple replies solemnly. "He's my father."

The puppet asks another question: "Who is Haja?" "Haja, is the Earth, nature itself," Maple replies. "She's the beating of every heart, the soul of our world; She's my mother." The puppet then asks, "What is your purpose?" Maple says, "My purpose in this life is to be a better human being every day; my purpose is to be a defender of nature, a protector of animals, to be the seed of positive change, and most importantly, my purpose is to have fun and be happy."

After a series of questions, the puppet asks a profound question: "Maple, what is the truth?"

Maple ponders for a moment and answers with certainty, "The only truth is love."

Dr. Goldbucket intervenes in the conversation and, as a professional, recommends that Maple continue her treatment. She hands her a business card from a colleague and suggests she reach out to him, assuring her that he can help her understand what's been going on in her mind.

After the impromptu session, the doctor bids a cordial farewell, and Maple is left alone with Pancake, reflecting on the questions Dinorah Goldbucket asked her through the puppet.

As Dr. Goldbucket left, Maple returned to her room and found the whale-shaped origami given to her by her hospital friend, Mpule, on her desk. She looked at the little piece of art closely, wondering if it had any deeper meaning, if it was one of the clues of Mister Universe. Curiosity suddenly got the better of Maple, who unfolded the paper to reveal a page from a mandala coloring book. Underneath the mandala were written the numbers 10:25. Maple smiled as she folded the origami again to its original shape and then looked at the photos Ashraf had given her.

Among the images, one particularly caught her attention: the tree. She looked at it carefully and suddenly noticed something familiar: it was the same tree she had seen inside the well on Haja Island. Then she looked at the other photo, the one that seemed abstract, and as she squinted, she saw Mister Universe's cat-like eyes. Maple smiled again. She lay back on her bed and closed her eyes; an indescribable peace came over her.

Suddenly, Mister Universe's voice echoed in the darkness: "Maple, are you ready? The adventure has just begun." Followed by the voice of Haja, who stated, "Rebirth is eternal, light is magical, and love is everything." Maple's heart pounded with happiness. In the darkness, Maple caught a glimpse of Thomas Woodfire, who was approaching her, and the surroundings lit up, revealing an untamed nature.

Maple opened her eyes and found herself in a white, padded wall room. A nurse came in and then out, leaving Maple deep in thought. The nurse turned to the doctor and said, "Dr. Woodfire, the patient is still immersed in a fantasy world, constantly talking about Mister Universe and Haja Island. She also keeps mentioning someone named Julie." With the sound of the key locking the door from outside, silence filled the room. Maple closed her eyes again, and Mother Haja held her in her arms.

∞

Glossary

Maple Pelridge: The protagonist of the story, deeply connected to nature and the universe, on a journey of self-discovery and spiritual awakening.

Honey Pelridge: Maple's sister, concerned about her well-being and actively involved in her life.

Julie Goldbucket: Maple's best friend, providing support and unique perspectives on her journey.

Dr. Dinorah Goldbucket: A psychologist who interacts with Maple, offering insights and guidance.

Scarlett: A mysterious woman with backward feet, whose significance remains enigmatic.

Thomas Woodfire: A character strangely connected to Maple, whose presence ignites curiosity and intrigue.

Pearl: Maple's mother, with whom she shares a significant and emotional connection.

Roman: Maple's father, with whom she shares a significant and emotional connection.

Lars: Maple's stepfather, who inspires Maple to do art.

Doris: Maple's grandmother, who has dementia.

Gaston: A character mentioned in the story, whose life takes a positive turn.

Ria: Maple's introverted and intellectual roommate.
Katie: A friend of Maple's from the hospital, providing support and understanding.

Mpule: A friend of Maple's from the hospital, who gifts her an origami whale.

Ashraf: A friend of Maple's from the hospital, who gifts her a book and some photos.

Danisa: Dr. Goldbucket's secretary.

Gleeter: Famous pop star and presenter of TV show Race for Fashion.

Jonah: Maple's ex-boyfriend, whose presence may still linger in her memories and experiences.

Pancake: Maple's dog.

Bagel: Julie's cat.

Marina Willows: Maples favorite place, an immense park in her city.

Fairy Forest: A nickname Maple came up with for a lush, forested area of Marina Willows with an enchanting energy.

The Serengeti: A nickname Maple came up with for a part of Marina Willows, evokes images of African plains in documentaries.

Cuervo Hills: Immersed in the Serengeti, deep in Marina Willows.

Haja Island: An island where Maple can find herself.

Mister Universe: A mysterious powerful entity encountered by Maple, influencing her worldview and beliefs.

Haja: The embodiment of nature and life.

Duck Lagoon: A part of Marina Willows, where Maple sees three turtles on a floating log.

Divination Cards: Cards Maple crafted herself, used for spiritual guidance, playing a significant role in her journey.

Overflowing Well: A mysterious well Maple encounters in Haja
Island.

145

Notes:

10:25